Echoes of Highland

A journey of faith, hope and change.

KIRAN BANTAWA RAI

BLUEROSE PUBLISHERS
India | U.K.

Copyright © Kiran Bantawa Rai 2025

All rights reserved by author. No part of this publication may be reproduced, stored in a retrieval system or transmitted in any form or by any means, electronic, mechanical, photocopying, recording or otherwise, without the prior permission of the author. Although every precaution has been taken to verify the accuracy of the information contained herein, the publisher assumes no responsibility for any errors or omissions. No liability is assumed for damages that may result from the use of information contained within.

BlueRose Publishers takes no responsibility for any damages, losses, or liabilities that may arise from the use or misuse of the information, products, or services provided in this publication.

For permissions requests or inquiries regarding this publication, please contact:

BLUEROSE PUBLISHERS
www.BlueRoseONE.com
info@bluerosepublishers.com
+91 8882 898 898
+4407342408967

ISBN: 978-93-7018-590-6

Cover design: Yash Singhal
Typesetting: Namrata Saini

First Edition: March 2025

Echoes of Highland

A Journey

of

Faith, Hope and Change

Dedication

I hold immense love and respect for the people of Sikkim—a community that embodies generosity, warmth, and kindness and emphasizes their shared values, culture and collective identity. Their traditions speak of resilience, faith, and a deep connection to their land.

Our culture is a tapestry of compassion, hospitality, and unity, where strangers become family and their literary heritage echoes the wisdom of the highlands.

This book, *Echoes of Highland: A Journey of Faith, Hope, and Change*, is a tribute to the inspiring people of Sikkim, India. It is for the mothers, fathers, elders, youth and children who carry forward their legacy with grace and hope. It is for every storyteller, student, teacher, and dreamer who calls Sikkim home.

Acknowledgement

I express my deepest gratitude to my beloved wife, family and friends, whose unwavering support and encouragement have been the absolute pillars of writing journey. Their patience, love, and belief in me have made this book possible.

Also, extend my heartfelt thanks to all those who have been part of this endeavor, directly or indirectly, offering guidance, support, motivation, and inspiration along the way. I'm truly blessed to have been able to work with you all.

Lastly, how can I forget my dear readers! A special thanks to my readers- your appreciation and encouragement for my previous book have really fueled my passion to write once again. Thank you for reading my books and sharing your valuable feedback! Every single feedback will help me correct myself and develop my writing career.

I was overwhelmed to have received various critical feedbacks of my previous book, 'A Dream's Death'. To be honest, most of the feedbacks were truly inspiring, heartwarming, motivational and encouraging ones for me. I'm blessed to have readers like you all.

This is for you.

A Note to My Readers

Dear Readers,

Writing '*Echoes of Highland: A journey of name, hope and change*' has been a journey of reflection, hope, and resilience. This book is not just a story—it is a tribute to the power of dreams, the strength of identity, and the relentless spirit of change. Through Myra's journey, I hope to capture the essence of struggle and transformation, not only at a personal level but also within the larger tapestry of society.

We all come from places that shape us—our roots, our values, and our people. The Highland in this story represent more than just a geographical setting; they embody the resilience of those who refuse to be defined by their circumstances. Myra's life is a testament to perseverance, proving that no dream is too distant when pursued with determination. From her childhood aspirations to her adulthood responsibilities, her journey is filled with moments of hope, disappointment, and self-discovery—just like many of us experience in our own lives.

One of the central themes of this book is the role of education—not just as a means of acquiring knowledge but as a force that transforms individuals and entire communities. Teachers, mentors, and guiding figures play an undeniable role in shaping the world, and this story is also a celebration of those who dedicate their lives to nurturing young minds. Myra's path to becoming a teacher wasn't an accident but a destiny shaped by inspiration and dedication.

Another key aspect of this story is change—both personal and societal. Progress is never easy. It comes with challenges, resistance, and sacrifices. The transformation of the Highland into a thriving place of opportunities mirrors the real struggles of any society aiming for growth. Through protests, debates, and the voices of people who dare to dream big, change is forged.

Politics, too, plays an inevitable role in shaping the lives of individuals. Whether we choose to acknowledge it or not, the policies and decisions made at different levels of leadership influence our daily realities. Good governance, ethical leadership, and informed citizens are crucial for a society's progress. I encourage you, dear readers, to not only engage with this story as fiction but to reflect on the real-world parallels it may hold.

Above all, this book is about hope—the kind that keeps us moving forward despite hardships. It is about the belief that every effort, every small step toward a better tomorrow, is meaningful. It is about the echoes we leave behind—our names, our actions, and the impact we have on others.

To those who dare to dream, to those who work tirelessly for a better future, and to those who believe in the beauty of change—this book is for you.

With heartfelt gratitude,

Kiran

Prologue

Everyone has a story, and life in the Highland was challenging for all. Today, many people recognize me – not just as a teacher, a proud mother, and a loving daughter, but also because my father is a renowned politician in Highland, the most beautiful state of the country. I am not a film star, sports legend or a Nobel laureate in any field, yet I know people would admire or recognize me more if I were one of them.

My name is Myra, and like everyone else, I have a story to tell.

I come from a small, middle-class family. I have a two-year-old daughter and a loving husband who serves in the Hindasia Army. I hold a simple degree in Arts from HGC. And yes, my small yet beautiful family lives in Rani Village, about 10 kilometres from Evergreen Marg, the breath-taking capital of the state.

For me, my parents are the greatest source of knowledge and experience in life. They are still young and dynamic in their own way, and I love them the most. I remember how I almost lost my dear father to a heart attack—an ordeal caused by the chaos and uncertainty in Highland. If I must place blame, it would be on politics.

My parents have taught me so many invaluable lessons—about struggle and fortune, distant relationships, the meaning of literature, and the true value of life.

My heart was pierced with a thousand wounds when I faced the kind of political turmoil that nearly destroyed my only dream profession. However, I fought with zeal and perseverance, pouring every ounce of my strength into healing my pain. I endured the suffering, bore the unbearable, and lived with courage and confidence—for my daughter, my husband, my beloved parents, and my society.

My mother has always been my guiding light. She taught me how to fight through highs and lows or rise and fall of life and to be bold and courageous enough to stand alone when needed. My father, on the other hand, is like a father to all—unchanging in his love, unwavering in his dedication. However, these days, he is a busy politician, tirelessly working day and night for the people of Highland. Still, he follows his daily routine with discipline, making him an exemplary figure for all.

"My father is perhaps the only father of the country," I often think, remembering my mother's childhood poem on 'Mother.' He embodies the qualities of a devoted father, a dynamic politician, and a true patriot. More than that, he is our protector and guide. The people of Highland admire him, showering him with praise on social media, TV, phone calls, and through print and digital media.

I often say, "Dad, you have the purest heart. You served in the Hindasia Army for years, and fate led you into politics, where you now serve the people with the same dedication.

You will forever be remembered in the political history of Highland." He smiles and says, "Politics requires a true patriotic spirit, and I believe I have some. I still remember how soldiers in the Hindasia Army suffered and lost their lives on the borders due to the so-called 'unethical or shadow politics' at the heart of centre. One cannot play politics at the boundary lines, for a single reckless decision can cost millions of lives."

My father never denies me anything. He simply smiles—his million-dollar smile—a smile that gives me strength to move forward.

Being an only daughter, I sometimes think, "I wish I had a sister." Perhaps she would have taught me how to love myself during my lowest moments, how to lean on someone in times of despair. I imagine she would be there for me in my darkest hours, reminding me that even in difficult times, life has a way of getting better.

Many times, I realize, "A sister understands a sister, and in my mother, I have found mine."

My father's career in the Army meant I couldn't spend much time with him as a child. He was posted across various states, primarily in the Northeast and Northwest of the country. He is a strong man with a great heart. My mother, on the other hand, was a devoted homemaker—a mother in the truest sense, a woman of strength and love. Perhaps that is why a mother is considered, the source of life.

God alone knows if I was born for a purpose—whether for someone who needed my presence, for a change that was destined to happen, or for a dream, I was yet to discover. I never knew if I was meant to be a teacher, to make a difference in society, or to bring about change in the educational or political systems of my state. But by the age of eleven or twelve, I had realized the power of education and the impact of a teacher. From then on, education became my passion.

I have always wanted to learn more—about happiness, life, love, education, politics, profession, and much more. I often wondered, even as a teenager, "Why is happiness so important? Why should life be meaningful?" I chose to seek those answers, to live a life of value, and to dream big.

There are people in our lives whom we love and rely on. Some may be on the verge of losing their jobs, finances, homes, friendships, or political or personal support. Yet, no matter what, they must remain courageous, even in the face of irreparable losses and political or personal crises. The dream I had nurtured for so long was almost shattered, had it not been for the values my parents instilled in me—the resilience to move forward and live a meaningful life.

Nani, my best friend, married to a teacher—Kishore Subba, a gentleman dedicated to his profession. He is a teacher at GSM School and is highly respected for his commitment to education and humanity.

People admire him for his cheerful nature, his knowledge, and the way he leads his life. Nani left her nursing job in Dream City, and they have now settled in Rani Village, remaining the best friend and neighbour I could ever ask for.

Anjali, Nani's daughter, is best friend with my daughter, Nidhi. They share a bond even stronger than the one Nani and I had during our childhood. Whenever Nani visits, we reminisce about our school days at APS, comparing our daughters' friendship to ours. We laugh, share memories, and never forget to mention Miss Sharma.

Today, I am a proud wife, a proud mother, and, most of all, a proud teacher. I teach at the Government Starlight Mission School in my village. Thanks to the new government, GSM School has been upgraded to 12th standard, with trained and qualified teachers, including myself. Perhaps the arrival of Miss Nidhi Sharma as a teacher was a blessing in disguise—a light of transformation in the lives of students, even if only for a year or so.

Life is not easy for me, but I fight every day to balance my professional and personal life. My profession is entirely different from my family's political life, which has remained stable for the past five years.

During odd hours, especially during the weekend, little Nidhi and I visit my grandparents' graves with flowers in our hands and love in hearts. My mother always told me that they never wanted to be separated; they believed in togetherness, eternal love, and humanity. Perhaps that is why God took them together. I wish I had met them at least once, but fate had another plan. Such is the law of nature—we are bound to accept it.

We return home with empty hands but tearful eyes. Mom misses her mother the most, and there is no way to comfort such a loss. We cannot teach our parents how to overcome grief, nor can we tell them, "Death is inevitable." The love of a parent for their own parents is unconditional, as pure as the snow-capped peaks of the Himalayas in Highland.

"Is it important to visit there every Weekend? Where are they now? Do they see us? Do they see the flowers we bring?" All these questions really troubled me until my late childhood. My dear mother would simply run her fingers over the tombstones in silent grief.

Sometimes, she wiped away her tears without letting me notice. She told me they were "sleeping forever" and had gone to heaven. But I still had more questions.

"How can we meet them in heaven?"
"We can't, not before we die."
"When will we die then?"
"I don't know, baby."

She rubbed her eyes. I noticed but said nothing. I hated seeing her sad. Instead, I turned my attention to the chirping birds nearby, trying to mimic their sounds.

"You are just like my sister," I once told her. And in that moment, I realized that I had, indeed, fulfilled her unspoken wish of having a sister.

I tell my little Nidhi, "Your grandparents love you to the moon and back," though she is too young to understand.

Everyone calls her "beauty with brains," "a Barbie doll," or "the Angel of Highland." But to me, she is simply my daughter—the one who inherited her grandfather's million-dollar smile.

Little Nidhi is the embodiment of Miss Nidhi's wisdom and inspiration.

And in honour of my teacher who had changed my life, I named my daughter Nidhi—a living reminder of the inspiration I once received. Every time she smiles, I silently whisper, "Thank you, Miss."

And with that, dear readers, it is time for a story.

Contents

1. Letters in Purple Envelope 1
2. New Beginning: Dreams and Dedication 14
3. A Day of Realizations 32
4. A Mother's Love 38
5. Lessons Beyond the Classroom 44
6. My Father, My Hero 50
7. The Challenges of Growing Up 55
8. The Legacy of Miss Nidhi 61
9. A Teacher Who Never Left (A Farewell to Remember) 66
10. The Weight of Goodbye (Healing And Growth) 76
11. A New Beginning: Behind The Facade 83
12. Echoes of Despair 90
13. A New Chapter, An Old Friend 98
14. The Unspoken Dilemmas or Bonds 109
15. Kesav and Myra: A Story Unfolding 121
16. Voices of the Forgotten 127
17. A Teacher's Calling 134
18. A Step Towards the Dream 141
19. Ties That Endure 153
20. Threads of Home and Hope 163

21. The Weight of Knowledge 173
22. A Dream Amidst Chaos 181
23. A Dream Fulfilled 187
24. The State's Transformation 196
Epilogue..204

1. Letters in Purple Envelope

That winter was the best one yet – a season wrapped in warmth despite the chill in the air. The streets and the pathways of Highland were dusted with soft snow, and every morning, I would wake up to the sight of delicate frost patterns on our windows. But what made that winter truly special wasn't just the beauty of the season—it was the time I spent with my mother, moments that became lifelong treasures.

Every shopping trip with her was an adventure. We would wander through the bustling market, my hands tucked into hers for warmth. She would patiently let me pick out my favourite woollen scarves and storybooks, smiling as I excitedly pointed at each new discovery. The joy of walking beside her, feeling her presence, and hearing her laughter made the cold days feel warm and bright.

The market was alive with the clatter of footsteps, the crisp air filled with the scent of roasted chestnuts. Mom and I walked hand in hand, my fingers wrapped in the warmth of hers. I tugged at the end of my scarf, watching in delight as vendors arranged colorful woollen shawls in neat piles. Everything felt festive, bright—until we passed a small tea stall where a group of men stood arguing.

One evening, as we strolled past a lively tea stall, a heated argument caught my attention.

"The new tax on fuel and vehicle is going to ruin us," one man said, his face flushed with frustration.

"They don't care about us," another replied, gesturing angrily toward the town hall. "They sit in their warm offices while we freeze out here."

I tugged at my mother's hand, curious. "What are they talking about, Mom?"

"Politics, Myra. Decisions made far away can change things for everyone, even here in Highland. But don't worry—these things have a way of working themselves out," Mom said sighing deeply.

Mom gave my hand a reassuring squeeze, leading me away from the rising tension. "Come on, Myra, let's see if they have the blue scarf you wanted." I nodded, letting my thoughts drift back to the warmth of the market. But somewhere deep inside, the weight of those men's voices lingered, a reminder that the world beyond my childhood wasn't always as simple as it seemed. Still, for now, my world remained safe, wrapped in my mother's warmth and my father's letters.

However, reading my father's letters and replying to him, miles away on duty, was yet another cherished moment during the vacation. I wanted to tell him everything—how much I missed him, how I was learning those meaningful words, and how I couldn't wait for his return.

And when his letters arrived, my mother would secretly keep them. We would sit by the fireplace, reading each word slowly, rubbing our eyes together, and cherishing the love in his handwriting. In those moments, he felt close, as if he were right there with us.

Exactly one week later, I woke up early, having seen my father in a dream. Perhaps the biting December wind had stirred something deep inside me. His absence was a void in our family, a reminder that we were incomplete without him.

Outside, the mist drifted slowly, and a light winter drizzle made the morning surprisingly cold. I pulled on my winter jacket and warm and soft woollen scarf before suggesting that Mom wear them as she had bought it just the previous week. She did not say a word—just looked at me, then smiled. The second time she smiled, she did not even look at me. Maybe she was lost in thought, realizing how quickly I was growing up.

"I did not mean to surprise you, Mom," I said.

She smiled again, broader this time. "I was just wondering if your dad were here."

I nodded. "Why isn't he coming home so often, Mom?"

"Duty is duty. And when it comes to an Army officer's duty, it's the toughest of all. You can't even imagine where he is right now or what dangers he faces. But he never lets me worry—never once has he told me how difficult it is."

I listened intently.

"He often tells me to take care of you—either through letters or over the phone. In the past, letters were our only means of communication. But now, thanks to technology, we can at least talk sometimes if not every time, considering his duty out there."

I listened even more closely.

"I have kept every one of his letters—they are my most precious treasures. Before you were born, they were my only company."

She looked at me, and I looked back. A million unspoken questions swirled in her eyes, but I had no answers, only questions of my own. Then, her expression changed, perhaps overwhelmed by the flood of memories. Without another word, she disappeared into the kitchen.

Left alone, I thought about Dad—his life, his sacrifices. Should I be proud to be the daughter of an Army officer, or should I regret that I had spent so little time with him?

A few moments later, Mom returned, carrying two cups of steaming tea.

"This will help with the cold," I thought.

I started drinking tea at a young age, maybe, because of the chilling cold in the Highland. Maybe, I had to accompany my dear mother, or maybe that was my taste of early life. I took my cup and sipped immediately. Mom's body language warned me to be careful, lest I burn my lips. I did not. She, too, took a sip, her expression hidden behind the cup's edge.

"Myra, let's get started," she said suddenly.

"What is it, Mom?" I asked, curious.

"Follow me," she replied with anticipation in her voice.

I followed her into a special room, one reserved for jewellery and other valuables. She carefully retrieved a beautiful box and placed it on the table.

"I don't think I've seen this before," I thought.

"That must be diamonds or some jewellery."

I was wrong. Inside were piles of letters—letters from my father, spanning over ten years.

"These are the true treasures of my life," Mom said as she carefully arranged them.

I stared at her in silence before helping her organize the letters by date. The envelopes came in many colors, but most were purple—Mom's favourite.

I couldn't stop staring at the purple ones.

"Color does matter in love," she murmured, setting those envelopes aside. I kept looking at them.

It would take me nearly a decade to truly understand what she meant. Eventually, purple became my favourite color too.

As Mom sorted through the letters, I remembered her visits to the post office, sending and receiving those envelopes. I realized that her love for the letters was more than just love for my father; it was a deep respect for an Army life, for a love that endured distance and time. But what struck me most was that my name appeared in nearly all the letters.

I longed to read them, "Could I possibly finish them all in just a day or two?"

"I have the entire vacation ahead of me," I reassured myself. "And, of course, Mom is here to read them with me."

"How many letters are there?" I asked, picking one from the middle of the stack.

"Forty-four," Mom answered without hesitation.

"How do you remember the exact number?" I asked, astonished.

"Love makes you remember everything," she replied with a soft smile and sat beside me.

I was still in disbelief. "How does she remember so precisely?"

"Do you want to read one?" Mom asked, her voice tinged with nostalgia.

I did not answer—I already knew I wanted to read them with her.

"You should read them all," she said gently.

I nodded and placed the letter back in the box.

"You need to understand your father—his life, his duty, his sacrifices."

I nodded again.

"Yes, Mom," I said, my excitement growing. "Let's read them."

As I reached for another letter, Mom stopped me.

"You should start from the first one," she insisted.

She wanted me to agree, and I did. She handed me a purple envelope from the very top of the pile she had just arranged.

Her warm smile reminded me why she was my mother—patient, wise and overflowing with love.

"Let's go outside," Mom said, putting the box back in its place.

"Okay, Mom," I replied, brimming with excitement.

I wasn't sure what I was anticipating more—the dream of my father or the chance to uncover his story.

She sat across the table, resting her chin on her hands, watching me. She was waiting for me.

Moving closer, I waited for her to read the letter. Something extraordinary was about to begin.

"Please read," Mom said.

"I want to hear it from you."

"I was waiting for you, though," I thought, smiling to myself.

I nodded happily, pulled the letter from its envelope, and saw that it was dated somewhere around 1990—a time before I was even born.

Mom's smile widened, encouraging me to begin.

It read:

My dear Divya,

I hope you are well.

I am so grateful to have you in my life, and I can't find the words to express my love and gratitude for you. You are my soul, my body, and my mind. Life in the Army is harsh in its own way, and I know you understand this. I endure the most brutal climates in the Himalayas and face the cruelest dangers in the border regions. Life here hardly feels like life at all.

Sometimes, I wish I were a teacher, sharing knowledge with thousands of students— living a life free of risks. But even so, I take great pride in serving my country as a soldier. Don't worry—I dream that our child, will become a great teacher one day.

I often think of my parents and yours, wishing they were still with us. If only that tragic accident hadn't taken them away...

If you ever need anything, I know our dear friend Madhu will always be there for you. Please convey my regards to her and her family.

The mountains around me are forever covered in snow, the air always is cold and heavy. Yet, every moment, I miss you.

My fingers are freezing now, and my pen is struggling to move.

Love,
Vikram
Army Camp, LOC, Snow Frontier.

I carefully placed the letter back exactly as it was, my father's images flashing through my mind. Mom took a deep breath and sighed heavily. Tears welled up in my eyes, and though I couldn't find the words to speak, I let them fall silently.

My father's handwriting was difficult to read sometimes, but I managed. Mom, equally overwhelmed with emotions, shared how she had wept each time she read his letters in the past.

"Reading his letters helped me escape the unbearable pain of missing him," she said, her voice trembling as she tried to suppress her sorrow.

A few drops of tears landed on the purple envelope. Before another could fall, I gently held both of my mother's hands.

"A sense of loneliness touched her," I thought.

"Dad, I love you," I whispered to myself.

"Your presence would have healed me, Dad," I thought, wishing he were there.

Wiping my tears, I looked into Mom's eyes and asked, "Mom, how did the accident actually happen?"

"They lost their lives in that 'fatal accident,' as your father mentioned in his letter, during a vacation tour about fourteen or fifteen years ago. We weren't married yet, but I had met your father just the year before that tragedy. Coincidentally, both my parents and your father's parents were on the same trip."

"That was about three years before I was born," I calculated in my head.

Mom continued, "We struggled immensely after losing our parents—facing hardships in education, health, happiness, and even our basic needs. But today, I'm grateful that we've managed to live with dignity."

Her words were yet another shock. Until then, I hadn't fully grasped the depth of our past. My young, curious mind always sought to understand things in detail.

"But, Mom…" I hesitated.

She anticipated my question and gently interrupted, "No one survived that accident." She knew that dwelling on painful memories wouldn't help us move forward. Leaving the past where it belonged seemed to be the best choice at that moment.

Having received my answer, I did not press further. I wanted to read another letter, but not that day. No more tears, not that day.

"We were both the only children of our parents," she added, her voice filled with a mother's wisdom and an unspoken understanding that I was beginning to feel her pain.

I simply listened. No more questions. Just silence.

Finally, she smiled through her tears and carefully placed the letter back in its envelope. I couldn't do it myself—not at that moment. Her gentle innocence overwhelmed me, and soon, we both smiled.

Outside, the sky darkened, and thunder rumbled. The wind howled, dark and heavy clouds racing across the sky, and then came the downpour—cold, relentless winter rain. We wiped our eyes and hurried inside our small kitchen. Standing by the only window, we watched hailstones pelt the ground like divine blessings. The raindrops shimmered, adding to nature's beauty. Only then did I truly realize how powerful nature was, its unpredictability mirroring our own lives.

Stretching out our hands, we tried to catch the falling hailstones, giggling as the icy fragments melted in our palms. It was in moments like these that Mom felt more like a sister or a friend than just a mother.

A few minutes later, she suddenly laughed and pointed toward the open porch. The purple envelope lay on the table, now covered in hailstones. I wanted to run and rescue it, but Mom quickly held my hands and stopped me. Instead, we laughed together, the hilarity of the moment breaking through our sorrow.

We missed Dad terribly that day, so we decided to write him a special letter that night.

From that day on, I read one or two of his letters daily. Mom helped me decipher his handwriting when I struggled. Through that winter, I learned more about his life, his profession, and his dream of becoming a teacher. Since then, I had only one wish—to make my parents proud.

Reading my father's letters made me feel like his real daughter. I realized that over and over again.

His words weren't just letters; they were pieces of him, woven into my childhood. And though he was far away, his presence lived within every page, every inked stroke, every unspoken promise.

By then, I had also begun speaking to Dad over the phone occasionally, either from home or through a PCO booth at the market. He always asked if everything was fine, but I never told him how deeply his letters affected me. I did not want to take up his valuable time. Sometimes, while talking, I could hear gunfire and explosions in the background. Before hanging up, he would always say, "Call you later, baby. I'm a bit busy. Give my regards to everyone out there especially, friends and take care of Mom and yourself."

Knowing that duty was duty, and that Army duty was the toughest of all, I would instantly end the call without protest.

I prayed every day for his safety but never told Mom about the gunfire I heard. I did not want her to worry.

Letters in Purple Envelope Summary

'Letters in Purple Envelope' paints a deeply emotional picture of a winter filled with warmth, love and longing. It also describes a poignant winter during Myra's childhood and the cherished memories despite the unbearable cold. Myra, a young girl reflects on special moments with her mother, such as shopping trips and reading letters from her father, an Army officer stationed far away. These letters, stored in a treasured box, reveal her father's sacrifices, his love for his family, and his pride in serving the country. A heated debate at a tea stall about rising taxes and government policies makes her realize that the world is far more complex than her childhood innocence had allowed her to see.

Through these letters, Myra begins to understand her father's life, his struggles, and his dreams, including his wish for her to become a teacher. The story also touches on the tragic loss of both her grandparents in an accident, which shaped her parents' lives. As the narrator reads the letters with her mother, she feels a deeper connection to her father and a growing sense of pride in his sacrifices.

The chapter ends with the narrator's resolve to make her parents proud and her silent prayers for her father's safety, as she begins to grasp the weight of his duty and the love that binds their family despite the distance.

2. New Beginning: Dreams and Dedication

Exactly twenty days later came one of the most exciting days of the year—my exam result. Nani, my best friend since kindergarten and I were both thrilled.

That morning, as we headed to school, excitement bubbling within us, we noticed a group of people gathered near the main road, holding placards. A young man raised his voice, "Save our trees! No highway through our forest!"

Nani, "They've been protesting for weeks now. Poor souls. But do you think anyone listens?"

I watched them for a moment. The protesters seemed determined, yet the passing cars barely slowed. "It's hard to say. Development always wins, doesn't it?" I replied, slightly confused.

Nani patted my shoulder. "Maybe. But sometimes, voices do make a lot of difference."

We walked on as the shouts of the protesters faded away behind us.

We arrived at school early that morning and waited eagerly at the entrance gate. As soon as the security guard unlocked it, we rushed toward the result board.

My best friend, the brightest girl in our class, and one of the most admired students in school, checked the results first.

After a moment of quiet reflection, I took a deep breath. The results were out.

No matter what they said, I reminded myself, I had given my best.

"You stood second, Myra!" she exclaimed. "Congratulations!"

"Thank you!" I smiled. "And what about you?"

I already knew the answer. No doubt. No question.

"First," she said, grinning.

"Congratulations!" I said, hugging her.

That moment of joy belonged to both of us. Our hearts swelled in pride. We had done it—we were at the top.

We also checked the notice board. School was set to re-open on *10th February, 2003*—just a week away.

During the day, one of my friends mentioned how the city was expanding fast. "Did you see those protesters this morning?" she asked. "I heard, they're still fighting to stop that new highway."

I recalled Nani's words. "Yeah. But will it matter to anyone? Will that make any difference?"

My friend shrugged. "True. But if they cut down all the trees, what happens to us?"

The question lingered in my mind. I thought of asking my mom, once in the evening. As the day went on, the conversation about the highway and the protesters kept surfacing in my thoughts. Would their voices really be heard? Would things change?

But for now, the warmth of companionship pulled me back to the present. As Nani and I walked home after school, laughter filled the air between us as we exchanged riddles, our eyes gleaming with excitement. The narrow pathway lined with wilderness in full bloom, their vibrant hues swaying gently in the breeze. Above the blooming wilderness, various kinds of birds chirped melodiously, flitting from branch to branch, their songs blending with the rustling leaves of nature.

We did not even realize how quickly we reached home. There, waiting for us, were our two mothers, chatting happily as they awaited their achievers.

"See, Divya, they're here," Madhu Aunt said, nudging Mom.

Mom, full of confidence as always asked, "So, what's the latest news?"

"We passed!" we shouted in unison.

Their proud smiles made us blush. For five whole minutes, we couldn't stop smiling under their affectionate praise. After all, we were their daughters and they had unwavering faith in us.

"We're so proud of you two, our dear daughters!" Madhu Aunt said, her voice filled with love.

"Thank you, Aunt," I said.

"Thank you, Mom," Nani echoed.

We were truly grateful to our supermoms.

"You did it!" they cheered.

Their happiness was evident in their eyes. To us, they were angels—guardians who watched over our health, education, dreams, and successes.

For a moment, I took in the warmth of the scene—our mothers' proud faces, the familiar comfort of home, and the quiet reassurance that we were supported.

"And as always, she's first, and I'm second," I chuckled.

Nani, blushed, nodding in agreement.

"Yes, you are right," Mom said, pride gleaming in her eyes.

"We're the luckiest ones," Nani whispered to me. I nodded, sharing her quiet happiness.

As our excitement settled, a warm sense of gratitude filled the room. Mom, smiling to herself, reached for the phone to share the good news with Dad. He was battling at the border—one of the most dangerous battlefields since World War II. Thankfully, we had a small Nokia phone, allowing us to reach him, at least sometimes.

The call did not go through at first. Mom tried five times before it finally connected. When she told him our results, his happiness was palpable. We excitedly took turns speaking with him.

His voice brimming with pride and joy. He congratulated both of us and even our mothers. For the first time, I saw Madhu Aunt visibly emotional.

Perhaps she was thinking of Uncle–Captain Thapa, her beloved husband–who laid down his life in the Snow Frontier War in 2002. It hadn't been that long ago. It had only been a year, and perhaps the loss of her husband still felt fresh.

Maybe she wished Nani's father could be here to share this moment.

Mom, sensing her silent grief, reached for her hand, offering quiet support. Without a word, Madhu Aunt nodded, acknowledging the unspoken bond between them. Nani and I watched them, admiring their lifelong friendship—one that had weathered both joy and sorrow. Without words, she nodded to Mom's support, just as she always did.

Dad's voice came through, breathless, as if he were deep in the Himalayas, struggling against the cold. For a brief moment, worry flickered in our eyes, but our two strong-hearted mothers reassured us with quiet confidence. A small smile crossed Madhu Aunt's face just as the call disconnected—another frustrating reminder of the poor network in those remote areas.

"It's okay, don't worry. He'll call back soon," Mom reassured us.

"Are you sure he's okay?" I asked unable to shake off the unease.

"It's just the network," Mom said. "That happens all the time in the Himalayas."

"I hope that's all it is…" I murmured more to myself than to anyone else.

Mom clapped her hands together, breaking the silence. "Now, what special treat shall we cook for you both tonight?"

We all exchanged glances and smiles, silently agreeing to let the super moms decide. They planned a special dinner, and we eagerly helped prepare some chicken *Momos*. After all, who could resist *Momos*, right?

The moment Mom mentioned Momos, our eyes widened with excitement. But just as quickly, Nani's smile faded.

Don't worry, Nani," Mom said with a knowing smile. "We'll make vegetarian ones just for you after the chicken." Nani's eyes lit up instantly, and her grin grew even wider than ours.

"High five!" I grinned, holding up hand.

"Yeah!" Nani laughed, slapping my hands with enthusiasm. Our palms met, and the happiness did not end there—it had only begun. Nani and I eagerly lent our innocent support to the process of making *Momos*.

The two super moms didn't join in, but their eyes sparkled with joy as they watched us. In that moment, it struck me—perhaps, being a mother isn't just about giving birth. It's about loving unconditionally, even when the child isn't your own.

After our much-anticipated dinner, our guests prepared to leave, but we wouldn't hear of it. With a little persuasion, they agreed to stay the night. That winter evening became one of the best we ever had—filled with laughter, warmth, and stories.
Just as we were settling in, the phone rang again. Dad was fine. Relief washed over us as we spoke, sharing every little detail of the night with him. We talked and talked until our eyes grew heavy. Nani and I slowly drifted off, while the two moms sat by the dim light, flipping through the fragile pages of Dad's letters. I don't know if they ever finished,

but in that quiet moment, they found comfort in each other's presence.

10th February, 2003

A week had passed since that unforgettable evening, but the joy still lingered in our hearts. The crisp winter air carried the scent of fresh earth as I made my way to school. Spotting Nani ahead, I quickened my steps.

"Good morning, Nani!" I greeted her cheerfully.

"Hi! Good morning." Her smile as bright as the morning sun.

"I'm so excited today—it's a new day, a new year, and a new class!"

"Me too!" she beamed.

We walked side by side, our footsteps crunching softly against the dirt path. After a moment, I mused, "I feel like we're not kids anymore."

"Yes, I feel the same." Nani nodded thoughtfully.

We walked together, and without realizing it, we had been holding our hands together. I had often heard people say, "Boys will be boys," but at that moment, I thought to myself, "Girls are just girls."

Once the assembly ended, excitement bubbled within me. Over the vacation, I had imagined so many possibilities—would any of them come true? Had I truly changed?

Our new classroom felt unfamiliar, almost foreign. I hesitated, unsure of which seat to choose, but Nani, ever decisive, pointed to the front row.

"Let's sit here," she suggested.

I nodded, and she smiled, pleased.

A good beginning leads to a good ending; I recalled my previous class teacher's words.

"Do you like this classroom?" she asked.

"Yes, I love it."

"What are you thinking?"

"As always…" I trailed off.

"And that is?"

"Good news. A good beginning."

Maybe she was right—I was always thinking about tomorrow, the future. Or perhaps I was simply aware of how life shifts, moment by moment, shaping us until the very end.

Nani nodded, settling beside me. She embraced every new start with ease. Intelligent, sincere, humble, and kind—she was the best friend I could have asked for. While she thrived in Science and Mathematics, my heart belonged to literature and history.

Just as we were chatting about our favourite subjects, the soft murmur of the classroom hushed. All eyes turned towards the door as a graceful woman stepped in.

"Good morning, class!"
"Good morning, Miss!" we chorused.

She wore a sleek watch and set a small pink bag on the table. There was something striking about her—her elegance, the way she carried herself.

"Class, my name is Nidhi Sharma, and I will be your English teacher."

To our surprise, many new students had joined, and the girls now outnumbered the boys. The classroom buzzed with noise.

Still smiling, Miss Nidhi picked up a chalk and wrote on the blackboard:

Class VII – Subject: English

She did not raise her voice, yet her presence commanded attention. Soon, noise faded into silence.

"Let's introduce ourselves," she said warmly.

"My name is Myra." I said. Then after a brief pause, I added, "Surname is Rai."

She smiled. "Beautiful name."

"Thank you, Miss."

"My name is Nani Thapa."

One by one, the students introduced themselves. Then, just when we thought introductions were over, Miss Nidhi surprised us with a game.

"Who knows the difference between 'Grammar' and 'Grammarian'?" she asked.

Silence!

Nani finally spoke. "Grammar is the rule of a language, and Grammarian is…" she hesitated.

I knew the answer –A Grammarian is an expert in Grammar– but I stayed quiet.

Miss Nidhi beamed. "Great answer!"

She explained further, her writing just as elegant as her presence. Soon, we all engaged in more mind games. The classroom echoed with laughter, and by the end of class, Miss Nidhi had already won our hearts.

During the break, Nani and I sat together discussing our new teacher.

"I liked her green watch and pink bag," I admitted. "She is so beautiful, and intelligent."

"What?" Nani smirked. "Oh, that?"

"Yes!"

"When you admire someone, you admire everything about them," I thought.

"Why do you like them so much?"

"I don't know," I shrugged.

She gave me thumbs up! "Let's get them one day."

I nodded, smiling.

Later that evening, during the assembly, Madam Principal, Rashi Roy, addressed us. My attention, however, was elsewhere – on Miss Nidhi, standing nearby, her green watch gleaming.

I had become her biggest fan in just one day.

On the way home, Nani teased, "You really liked that watch, huh?"

"Not just liked—I loved it."

"One day, I'll become a great teacher and buy one."

"Okay," she grinned. "Let's do it."

Back home, Mom was cooking dinner, singing an old Highlander song in her beautiful voice. I thought about mentioning the watch but changed my mind.

"I don't want to trouble her. She's the best mother," I thought.

I attempted some math problems but soon found myself sketching squirrels and some raccoons. My mind was restless.

"Is everything alright at school, Myra?" Mom asked.

"Yes! And I have good news!"

"What is it?"

"A new teacher! She's so beautiful, intelligent, and – she is our class teacher too!"

Mom's eyes lit up. "That's great wonderful! What's her name?"

"Nidhi Sharma. And she has this gorgeous green watch and a pink bag."

Mom laughed and said, "Sounds like you admire her a lot."

"And her handwriting! It's like an art."

She chuckled again. "Maybe one day, my daughter will be a great teacher like her."

I nodded, feeling warmth spread through me. "Thank you, Mom."

She hugged me, filling me with warmth. That night, as I studied, read with Mom, I listened to her wisdom.

Later, as we sat by the fireplace, our only radio crackled with the voice of a news anchor. The report was about a recent decision by the state government to build a new highway through Rani Village in Highland.

"The project promised to bring economic growth," the anchor said, "but many locals are concerned about the impact on the environment and their homes."

I looked at her and asked, "What do you think, Mom?" She paused, and her hands were still. "It's complicated, Myra. The highway could bring jobs and better roads, but it might also harm the forests and the animals. Sometimes, progress comes at a cost."

My heart sank. I thought of the protesters from the morning, their determined faces and the stories my father told about the beauty of Highland's wilderness. I wondered if there was a way to have both—progress and preservation.

Education, she always emphasized, was the key to everything, especially for women. I admired her strength—

she had pursued learning despite poverty. Her story inspired me, and for the first time, I realized literature would shape my future.

One day, I thought, I will tell stories too.

Later that night, she sat by her bedside and read some of her favourite poems. One of them was "A Valediction Forbidding Mourning" by John Donne. It was perhaps, written at the beginning of the 17th century. I was astonished to see her deep love for poetry of all kinds, especially English poetry. Until that day, I never knew she was fond of poems or that she had collected so many books of poetry. As she finished reading, I noticed something—Mom wiped her eyes, and her tears drifted down her face like a small brook making its own way towards the oceans.

"I wanted to study. I wanted to become a great philosopher or a writer. However, I couldn't carry my further studies forward due to financial constraints and my own family background," I recollected Mom's words from the past.

"She probably missed Daddy," I thought. Knowing she was in pain, I asked her if she was okay. She nodded her head.

"I'm fine," she said, reaching for my hands. She held me close. I felt the absence of my Daddy—my mother's adored husband—especially in moments like these, when her tears reflected either the love of happiness or the sorrow of longing.

"My mother could have been a good teacher," I thought as I looked at her.

"You're my inspiration," I said.

She nodded again, this time with a broad smile.

"I'm okay, Myra," she said. "I just missed your Daddy through this poem."

"I was correct," I thought, slightly smiling but without saying a word.

I knew Daddy had sent so many letters in the past. Now, I recalled some photographs of his Army life. Some of the photographs were kept in various black and white frames and a few in colored ones, each capturing a different moment of his journey. Mom took one out from the middle of a small Almirah—perhaps something only the wives of Army men had around that time. She ran her fingers over the picture more than a couple of times. Missing him in desperation, she kissed the photograph, then me, longing filling her eyes. Again, she hugged me and kissed my forehead.

Meanwhile, she arranged everything properly before going to bed. Mom was meticulous in her efforts, no matter what she did—the best Mom any child could have on this planet. I felt pity for her, being far away from my dear father. Moreover, I felt pity for her fortune and life, but I did not know why. But she wasn't, at all. Maybe that was her strength—enduring pain with grace, turning wounds into wisdom and love into an unshakable foundation.

I was flipping through some old letters and a few photographs when Mom's voice broke the silence, "It's bed time."

"Okay, Mom," I replied, sensing that she was at ease now.

As I got up, I remembered something, "I have to brush my teeth."

She smiled. "That's great! You have to protect your teeth from cavities."

"Not just cavities, Mom," I said. "Brushing has so many benefits."

"Umm… I see," she said, amused. "Good daughter."

"Thank you, Mom."

"Let me get some warm water for you."

"Okay, Mom."

We had lost track of time– Mid midnight had crept upon us.

Mom returned, placing a covered glass of water on the table, "Here's your water."

"Thanks Mom."

"Welcome… welcome," she sang softly, making up her own tune as she pulled the blanket over me and kissed my forehead again.

"Myra," she said. "Put off the light, baby."

"Okay, Mom."

"Good night, Myra."

"Good night, Mom," I whispered groping for the switch.

I closed my eyes, feeling the warmth of the blanket around me. My body relaxed, and my thoughts slowly blurred into dreams.

Suddenly, I found myself in the classroom. It was a bright and beautiful day. The sun was shining, and its rays entered the classroom through small windows. Miss Nidhi walked into the class. But something was different – her wrist watch was bare, the pink bag was missing. I frowned and wondered why? My curiosity surged.

"Good morning, Miss," we greeted her together.

"Good morning," she replied cheerfully with all her grace.

"Please, take your seats."

I looked at her as she wrote on the board:

"G-R-A-M-M-A-R – the basic rules of a language."

"Grammar is a system or a basic rule of any language," she explained. "It is also the beauty of a language, as it makes any language beautiful when spoken correctly."

She asked questions to everyone, and I did not ignore hers.

"I have already learned about Grammar," I said. Some of my friends giggled.

"Silence, please!" she said firmly.

The best answerer got a prize, but everyone enjoyed chocolates. We were asked to sing songs. Nani was called first. At once, she flinched, looking at me with wide eyes, but she showed no sign of nervousness. She walked to the front of the class and sang a song or two. I found her more confident than everyone else, even me. Everyone applauded, and Miss Nidhi joined in.

"Thank you," Nani said as she blushed and finished her song.

"I wish I could sing like Nani," I thought. I, had a deep love for music and dance, though I wasn't as skilled as Nani. After a while, we all joined in with equal enthusiasm, letting our hearts lead where our steps sometimes faltered.

"Let's give her a big round of applause," Miss Nidhi said, and a huge round of applause followed. More students participated. Miss Nidhi encouraged and congratulated us, thanking all for their participation.

"Thank you," she said with a broad smile.

At times, I felt like I was in the middle of an APS choir.

"I encourage you all to participate more. Learning from one another is vital to moving forward efficiently. Every child is special in his or her own way, and participation is everything. That is education."

"Yes, Miss!" the whole class shouted together. It was a joyous moment.

Then she said, "Let's do the final Roll call now."

"Roll no. 1?"

"Yes, Miss!" I called out and – woke up, panting.

Mom, sleeping next to me, woke up, startled.

"Are you alright, Myra?" she asked, her voice filled with concern.

"I gasped for breath," It…it can't be just a dream."

I could still hear the clapping; feel the excitement, "How can a dream be so real?"

Mom comforted and wrapped her arms around, drawing me closer.

"It's just a dream, Myra. Don't worry," she said.

I nodded, trying to calm down. Eventually, I fell asleep again.

New Beginning: Dreams and Dedication

Summary

'New Beginning: Dreams and Dedication' begins with the narrator, Myra and her best friend, Nani, eagerly awaiting for their exam results. Both achieve top ranks, bringing immense pride to their mothers.

Myra's father, an Army officer stationed at the Snow Frontier border, shares in their joy during a heartfelt phone call. The chapter also highlights the emotional bond between the narrator's mother and Nani's mother, Madhu, who lost her husband in the Snow Frontier War, in 2002.

As the new school year begins, Myra and Nani meet their inspiring English teacher, Miss Nidhi Sharma, whose elegance and passion for teaching spark the Myra's dream of becoming a teacher. The chapter ends with a tender moment between Myra and her mother, reflecting on their love for the narrator's father and the sacrifices of Army life, while also celebrating the power of education and dreams.

3. A Day of Realizations

The next morning, I awoke to the sound of birds chirping outside my window. Their melodies were soft yet insistent, as if urging the world to rise and embrace the day. I lay still for a moment, listening to their symphony, and wondered what it would be like to be one of them—free, weightless, and unburdened by the constraints of human life.

"What a breezy morning!" I thought, stretching lazily under the warmth of my blanket.

For a fleeting moment, I imagined myself as a bird, soaring through the endless sky, flying to where my Daddy was stationed. I would see him, hug him, and then return home and before anyone noticed I was gone. But as quickly as the fantasy came, it faded. I knew better. Some dreams remain just dreams, and this was one of them.

A couple of hours later, Mom's voice broke through my reverie. "It's now 8:30 a.m.," she announced, her tone calm but firm.

I glanced at the clock, realizing time had slipped away, she was right. Hurriedly, the kitchen hummed with the rhythm of our morning ritual, my hands moving in sync with hers as we packed my tiffin. After dressing in my uniform, panic struck—my English book was missing.

Frantically, I searched my room, anxiety mounting as Madam Rashi's stern warnings and Nidhi Miss's inspiring presence loomed in my mind. Just as despair set in, Mom found it under my pillow. Relief turned to embarrassment, then gratitude as I hugged her tightly. Her stern yet affectionate look reminded me to be more careful.

In that moment, I realized my panic wasn't just about the book—it was about my deep respect for learning and my teachers. Nidhi Miss, with her grace and inspiration, embodied everything I aspired to be. Missing her class or failing to meet her expectations felt unthinkable. This was more than a search for a book; it was a realization of how much I valued education and the opportunities it offered. Perhaps this was the moment I truly understood the importance of learning in shaping my future.

"Let's go," Mom said, breaking my train of thought.

"Okay, I'm ready," I replied.

She picked up my school bag, but I gently stopped her. "Mom, I can carry it myself from now on."

She looked at me with surprise and a hint of pride. I held her left hand and walked besides her, feeling the warmth of her touch. Little did I know that this was perhaps the last day she would be dropping me off at school. From that day onwards, I would miss her presence every morning.

"Yes, I am no longer a little girl," I thought to myself as memories of our walks to school over the years played in my mind. I remembered how she used to hold my hand tightly, her grip firm yet reassuring, as we navigated the bustling streets. I remembered the stories she would tell me—stories of courage, resilience, and love—that shaped my understanding of the world. And I remembered the way she would wave goodbye, her smile a beacon of comfort as I stepped into the school gates.

On the way, we met Nani and her mother. We exchanged greetings and continued walking together. As we approached the school, I observed how many students came alone, carrying their heavy school bags, umbrellas, and even looking after their younger siblings. That day, I truly realized how challenging school life was for some students who lacked parental support and financial stability. The government was working hard to eradicate poverty and build an educated, prosperous society, but there were still many children who had to shoulder responsibilities beyond their years.

Some students did not even have parents. They had to take care of themselves, manage their studies, and navigate life's difficulties alone. Life wasn't easy for them. Education, under such circumstances, was an enormous challenge.

Finally, we arrived at school. I saw my friends playing on the ground, their laughter filling the air. Both our mothers turned to leave after dropping us off.

"Bye, Myra," Mom said as she waved at us and walked back home with Madhu Aunt.

"Bye, Mom!" I waved at them. "Please manage yourselves in the evening with Nani."

"We're girls now," I thought, and nodded confidently.

Our mothers exchanged amused glances, while Nani and I looked at each other knowingly. They might not have realized it yet, but we were stepping into our teenage years. A change was happening, even if they did not acknowledge it yet.

As I walked into school, a thought lingered in my mind: How lucky we were to have our mothers by my side—so caring, so loving.

"Mothers are the true connoisseurs of love, truth, life, death, birth, struggles, science, literature, and almost everything. They are the creators and protectors of this world. A mother's love is the love of God, of family, of society—it completes a full circle, just like in mathematics. To me, a mother is a divine entity, a true creator of humanity and truth," I thought.

I recalled then, one of my teachers' words, "It's wonderful to see how much you have matured in your thinking and perspectives." I didn't know if I was in my reverie.

But life was always changing, wasn't it? Just like the seasons, just like the years slipping past us. "One day, we are holding our mother's hand tightly; the next, we are learning to stand on our own." And beyond our personal worlds, change was happening everywhere—sometimes quietly, sometimes with a storm.

That evening, as the town came alive with the colors and sounds of the festival, I couldn't help but wonder about the changes unfolding around us.

One of our local festivals was in full swing, Nani and I were joined by our parents in the celebrations here in Evergreen. The celebration was full of music, laughter, and the enticing entertainments. But as we walked past a group of elders gathered under a sprawling banyan tree, a conversation caught our attention, making us pause.

"The new leader is going to bring change," one of them said.

"Change for whom?" another replied bitterly. "The rich get richer, while the rest of us continue to struggle."

I glanced at Mom, who gave me a reassuring smile. "Don't worry, Myra. These are just conversations. People have been saying things like this for as long as I can remember in Highland." I could see Nani and Madhu Aunt nod at each other.

Still, I couldn't shake the feeling that something was shifting in the state. The joy of the festival felt bittersweet—a reminder that even in moments of celebration, the challenges of life were never too far away.

A Day of Realizations Summary

Myra begins her day with a reflective moment, listening to the morning birds and imagining the freedom of flight, wishing she could visit her father stationed far away. As she prepares for school, a brief panic over a misplaced book reminds her of her deep respect for education and her teachers.

Walking to school with her mother, she realizes how fortunate she is to have her by her side. Observing other students who face struggles without parental support, she gains a newfound appreciation for the privileges she often took for granted. A thought lingers in her mind—mothers are not just caregivers but the foundation of love, wisdom, and resilience.

Later that day, Evergreen comes alive with the colors and sounds of a local festival. Myra, Nani, and their parents immerse themselves in the joyous atmosphere, but a conversation among elders under a banyan tree shifts her perspective. Talks of change and inequality make her reflect on how the world is evolving around her. Though the festival is a time of celebration, she senses an undercurrent of uncertainty, realizing that change—whether in her own life or in society—is inevitable.

4. A Mother's Love

The school auditorium buzzed with excitement as students hurriedly pinned paper flowers onto their uniforms. It was Mother's Day, and for the first time, I would be celebrating it at APS with Nidhi Miss.

The event was grand, with dignitaries gracing the occasion and a gathering of students, teachers, and parents. The school auditorium was adorned with colorful decorations, and the air carried the scent of fresh flowers and the hum of excited chatter.

I could see Nani sitting by her mother's side, close to where I was. However, my mom wasn't there. She had a doctor's appointment that couldn't be rescheduled. As I sat among my classmates, her absence weighed heavily on me. Every time a mother stepped onto the podium to share her thoughts, my heart ached a little more. I thought, 'Life is first, and everything else is secondary.'"

The speeches were deeply moving, narrating stories of sacrifice, love, and resilience. One mother spoke about how she had worked multiple jobs to ensure her children could attend school. Another shared how she had supported her daughter through a serious illness, never leaving her side. Each story was a testament to the strength and selflessness of mothers, and I found myself nodding along, my admiration was growing with every single word.

Yet, amidst the applause and the heartfelt moments, I couldn't shake the feeling of emptiness. I missed my mom terribly. I wished she could have been there to hear the stories, to feel the love and appreciation that filled the room. I wished I could have stood up and spoken about her—about her unwavering support, her endless patience, and the quiet strength that held our family together.

That evening, as the birds chirped and frogs croaked, I sat at my desk, trying to focus on my homework. The events of the day played in my mind, and I found it hard to concentrate. Mom, as usual, was busy in the kitchen, her voice drifting in from the other room as she talked on the phone. The familiar sounds of her movements—the clinking of utensils, the soft hum of her voice—were a comfort, but they also reminded me of how much I had missed her presence earlier in the day.

After a while, she came to check on me, ensuring I was studying and had completed my assignments. Her presence was calming, and I felt a wave of gratitude wash over me.

"Mom," I called, seeking her attention.

She looked at me seriously. "Is there a problem?"

"No," I reassured her. "I just have a question."

She smiled warmly, the kind of smile that could light up even the darkest room. "No matter what, Myra. I am always here for you. Chase your dreams, live with love and courage—your father and I believe in you," she said. "Everyone believes in you," she added.

Her words touched me deeply, and I felt a lump form in my throat.

"Mom," I said, my voice softening. "As you know, today was Mother's Day. I missed you so much. I wish I could have given you something special."

She held my hands gently, her touch warm and reassuring. "You are my gift," she replied, her eyes filled with love.

Tears welled up in my eyes as she continued, "I don't need anything more than you. Just be yourself, be a good daughter, and that will be the greatest gift of my life."

I simply nodded, overwhelmed with emotion. Her words were a balm to my soul, a reminder of the unconditional love that had always been my anchor.

"What was it that you wanted to ask me?" she prompted, her voice gentle.

I hesitated for a moment, gathering my thoughts. The question had been weighing on my mind all day, and now, in the safety of her presence, I felt ready to ask it.

"Mom, what is a mother's love?" I asked, though I already knew a little as a growing daughter.

She looked thoughtful, her gaze drifting to the window where the evening light was fading. Instead of answering immediately, she reached for her diary, a well-worn book that held her thoughts, dreams, and reflections. She opened it to a fresh page and began writing.

As she wrote, I watched her, marveling at the way her hand moved across the page with such purpose and grace. When she finished, she handed the diary to me, and I read her words:

A Mother's Love

"A mother's love is eternal,
A sacrifice beyond measure,
A power that heals pain,
A force that nurtures dreams.
It is unconditional, pure, and boundless,
It instills patience, strength, and kindness,
It teaches respect, humility, and love.
A mother is the light of a home,
Her laughter, a melody of joy,
Her tears, a whisper of warmth,
Her love, an unshaken pillar,

The foundation upon which life stands."

As I read her words, I felt a deep sense of awe and gratitude. Her love wasn't just a feeling; it was a force, a guiding light that had shaped me in so many ways. I was only beginning to understand what life and love truly meant.

That night, as I lay in bed, I thought about the day and the lessons it had brought. I thought about the mothers who had shared their stories, about the sacrifices they had made, and about the love that had carried them through. I thought about my own mother, her quiet strength, her endless patience, and the love that had always been my safe harbor.

I realized that a mother's love wasn't just about the big moments—the celebrations, the gifts, the grand gestures. It was in the everyday things—the way she checked on my homework, the way she held my hand, the way she smiled even when she was tired. It was in the way she believed in me, even when I doubted myself.

As I drifted off to sleep, I felt a profound sense of peace. I knew that no matter where life took me, I would always carry her love within me—a love that was eternal, pure, and boundless. A love that was the foundation of my life.

A Mother's Love Summary

On Mother's Day, the school auditorium buzzes with excitement, but Myra feels a void—her mother couldn't attend due to an unavoidable doctor's appointment. As she listens to heartfelt speeches about maternal love and sacrifices, she longs for her mother's presence, realizing how much she means to her. That evening, surrounded by the familiar comforts of home, Myra shares her feelings with her mother, who reassures her with a simple yet profound truth: Myra herself is the greatest gift a mother could ask for.

Touched by her mother's words, Myra asks what a mother's love truly means. In response, her mother pens a heartfelt poem, describing a mother's love as eternal, selfless, and the foundation of life. As Myra reads the words, she gains a deeper understanding—love isn't just in grand gestures but in everyday moments of care and belief. That night, as she reflects on the day, she finds peace, knowing that no matter where life takes her, her mother's love will always be with her.

5. Lessons Beyond the Classroom

A few months later, in the afternoon, the sun streamed through the windows of APS, casting long, golden shadows across the classroom. The air was warm and still, carrying the faint scent of chalk dust and the rustling of pages as students flipped through their notebooks. Miss Nidhi stood by the blackboard, her silhouette framed by the soft glow of sunlight. Her gentle but firm voice filled the room, each word deliberate and weighted with meaning.

"Failure is not the end," she said, her eyes scanning the rows of students. "It is only a lesson in disguise."

I sat in the first row, my fists clenched tightly under the desk. My maths test paper lay in front of me, the red marks glaring back like accusations. I had barely passed. The numbers blurred before my eyes, and a heavy knot of shame settled in my chest. I could feel the heat rising to my cheeks, and I kept my gaze fixed on the desk, afraid to meet anyone's eyes.

Sensing my distress, Miss Nidhi walked over, her footsteps soft but purposeful. Without a word, she slid a book onto my desk. "Read page 33," she whispered, and marked by a folded page in the middle of that book, her voice carrying a knowing smile. Then she moved on, leaving me with a flicker of curiosity amidst my disappointment.

That evening, as the sun dipped below the horizon and the sky turned a deep shade of orange, I sat on my bed with the book in my hands. The house was quiet, except for the distant hum of my mother's voice in the kitchen. Curious, I flipped to page 33 and began to read:

"The greatest minds in history—Albert Einstein, Thomas Edison, even Abraham Lincoln—faced failure over and over again. But they never gave up. Because perseverance, not perfection, shapes true success."

The words struck a chord deep within me. I read them again, letting them sink in. For the first time, I felt a glimmer of hope. Maybe my failure wasn't the end of the world. Maybe it was just a stepping stone, a lesson waiting to be learned.

The next day, I stayed back after school, my heart pounding as I approached Miss Nidhi's desk. She was grading papers, her pen moving swiftly across the pages. I hesitated for a moment, then cleared my throat.

"Miss," I said, my voice trembling slightly, "do you really think I can get better?"

She looked up, her eyes warm and encouraging. "I don't just think, Myra. I know."

Her words were like a balm to my bruised confidence. She spoke with such conviction, such unwavering belief, that I couldn't help but believe her.

In that moment, I made a silent promise to myself: I would work harder. I would prove to her—and to myself—that I was capable of more.

Years later, as I stood before my own students, I often found myself thinking about the teacher who once changed my life. Every time I saw a struggling child, I remembered the silent applause of encouragement Miss Nidhi had once given me. And, just like my idol teacher, I passed it on forever.

When I was in the 7th standard at APS—Army Public School, East Highland—I had the privilege of being taught by Nidhi Miss. She wasn't only my English teacher but also my class teacher for around one year or so. That was how I met Nidhi Sharma, the teacher who became my favourite and left an everlasting impact on my life. She played a crucial in inspiring my dream of becoming a teacher. The moral values she instilled in her students, including me, were unforgettable and praiseworthy, especially for someone like me who came from a lower-middle-class background.

I have vivid memories of my time with Nidhi Miss in school—her unique teaching methods, the engaging games she played with students of all kinds, and the values she imparted. She taught me the importance of hard work, honesty, love, respect, compassion, and forgiveness—virtues that are essential in life. She always emphasized that love and kindness were just as important as academic excellence, if not more. Education wasn't merely about obtaining degrees; it was about shaping one's character and making a difference in the world. This lesson remained with me throughout my life.

Today, people know me as Myra, once a beloved student of Miss Nidhi Sharma, an esteemed English teacher at APS. I hail from a small but beautiful Himalayan state in Hindasia called Highland. Nepali is the lingua franca of the region, although numerous local languages are spoken all across the state. Over the years, English has gained prominence and is now widely spoken and understood across the state.

Growing up in Highland, I learned that education was more than just academics—it was about shaping one's character. Miss Nidhi instilled in us the virtues of hard work, kindness, and perseverance—principles that resonated deeply in our small but beautiful Himalayan state. I always thought our state was peaceful, but sometimes, I heard people say things weren't fair. I didn't understand what they meant, but it made me wonder—if everyone wanted things to be better, why didn't they change? While our people thrived on unity, some leaders took advantage of this peace for personal gain. I often heard grown-ups talk about politics, about leaders who made promises but never kept them. I didn't understand everything, but I could tell that not everyone was happy with the way things worked.

Our people had a rich history, distinct customs, vibrant cultures, and deep-rooted traditions. Most importantly, they had lived in harmony, which was why our state was often regarded as a beacon of peace. Perhaps it is this very harmony that attracts thousands of domestic and international tourists to our homeland every year. Many parts of our state have long been famous tourist destinations, drawing visitors who admire our state's breath-taking beauty, tranquillity, and sense of unity.

Tourists frequently praised Highland for its mesmerizing landscapes, peaceful environment, and communal harmony. I always loved how people in Highland treated everyone like family. But once, I heard an old shopkeeper tell my mother, "Tourists come and go, but our lives don't change." I didn't understand what he meant at the time, but his words stayed with me. Perhaps it was this welcoming nature that made tourism one of the state's major sources of income.

Yet, despite this serenity, politics remained a complex force, often shaping or affecting lives in unseen ways. Politics exerted a strong influence over people's lives, sometimes in ways that are not entirely fair or beneficial. Some political leaders had, at times, taken advantage of the state's peaceful environment for their own gains. Sometimes, I wondered who really made the rules—was it the leaders, the people in courts, or just the grown-ups who made all the decisions? I didn't have the answers, but I knew that not everyone agreed on what was right. An ordinary citizen couldn't always comprehend the full extent of these complexities. Many remained unaware of such issues, and life simply carried on.

Lessons Beyond the Classroom Summary

Myra, a young student at APS, struggles with failure after a disappointing maths test. Her teacher, Miss Nidhi, recognizes her distress and silently offers her a book, marking a passage about perseverance. As Myra reads about great minds who overcame failure, she begins to see her struggles differently. Encouraged by Miss Nidhi's unwavering belief in her, she resolves to work harder, a lesson that stays with her for life. Years later, as a teacher herself, Myra carries forward the same encouragement and wisdom she once received.

Reflecting on her time in Highland, Myra realises that education is more than just academics—it shapes one's character. She recalls the unity and peace of her homeland but also the political undercurrents that often went unnoticed. Though she was too young to fully understand, she sensed the gap between promises and reality. The welcoming nature of her people made Highland a thriving tourist destination, yet behind the beauty, life for ordinary citizens remained unchanged. As she grew, so did her awareness of the deeper complexities of the world around her.

6. My Father, My Hero

As days turned into months and months into years, I gradually gained a deeper understanding of my father's profession. The uniform he wore with such pride, the medals that gleamed on his chest, and the determined look in his eyes were all symbols of the sacrifices he made for the country. My father, Major Vikram Rai, had dedicated more than a decade of his life to the Hindasia Army—a journey filled with hardships, unwavering commitment, and immense courage. His recent promotion to Major was a recognition he truly deserved.

Even as a child, I could sense that Snow Frontier was never a place of comfort for an Army officer. It was a land of unforgiving weather, relentless enemies, and constant danger. Unlike other fathers who returned home from work every evening, mine could only visit once or twice a year. His presence at home was rare, but his absence was a constant void in my heart. I often sat by the window, reading his letters, tracing the inked words with my fingers, feeling his emotions woven into every line. Sometimes, a tear would escape my eyes as I longed for his embrace, his reassuring voice, and the stories he would tell me about his life at the border.

In one of his letters, my father wrote:

"Highland is a beautiful place, Divya, but it's also a place of contradictions. The people here

are strong and resilient, but they face many challenges—poverty, lack of resources, and sometimes, leaders who don't listen. I hope that one day, Myra will be part of the change this place needs."

I read that letter over and over, my father's words stirring something deep within me. For the first time, I began to see Highland not just as my home, but as a land with its own struggles and dreams.

I loved him so much that I wished we could live together permanently, but that was impossible. He had a duty—a duty that came before everything else. The nation needed him, and he had sworn to protect it, even at the cost of his own life.

My mother always reminded me, "For a soldier, the nation comes first, before his family and society." Those words, though simple, carried the weight of immense sacrifice. It was a truth we had learned to live with.

Whenever my father returned home, our house transformed into a place of celebration. Neighbours, relatives, and friends would gather, eager to hear his stories, each tale filled with the thrill of battles, the camaraderie among soldiers, and the indomitable spirit of the Army. Sometimes, his stories left us in awe; other times, they made our hearts race with fear.

I often thought to myself, "All credit goes to my dear Dad, the only true gentleman in my eyes."

Through him, I learned about the harsh realities of Army life, especially the hardships soldiers endured at the Snow

Frontier Border. The more I listened, the more I understood that their challenges were far beyond what any civilian could imagine.

"We don't just fight enemies; we also battle nature," my father once said with a deep sigh.

His words painted a vivid picture of the frozen battlefield where he was stationed—the highest battleground in the world, standing at nearly 20,000 feet. The temperature there plummeted to a bone-chilling minus (-50) degrees Celsius.

The air was so thin that even breathing became a struggle. Snowstorms raged unpredictably, and the biting winds could slice through even the thickest of Army gear.

"At Snow Frontier, rations are air-dropped by helicopters," he explained. "Do you know, fruits like apples and oranges freeze solid within moments of being exposed to the air?"

I imagined the soldiers, my father among them, breaking off pieces of frozen fruit, their fingers numb from the cold, their bodies aching but their spirits unyielding. The thought filled me with both pride and sorrow.

The more I learned, the more I worried about my father's safety. Every time a news report mentioned clashes at the border, my heart would pound with fear. Yet, my mother never let her worries show. Perhaps she had mastered the art of suppressing her fears, knowing that breaking down was never an option. She was a soldier's wife, a woman of remarkable strength who carried the weight of both love and sacrifice on her shoulders.

Gradually, I realized that she wasn't just any woman—she was a pillar of resilience. She loved my father deeply, just as she loved our family and our country. Often, I would overhear her whisper to him on the phone, reassuring him, "Don't worry about us. We are fine. Just take care of yourself."

Perhaps she knew that if she showed the slightest sign of weakness, it would only burden him further. And so, she remained steadfast, standing tall like a silent guardian, holding our home together in his absence.

As I watched my mother's steady hands fold my father's letters, her quiet strength mirrored his bravery on the battlefield. My chest swelled with a pride I couldn't put into words.

Education was something they never compromised on. Even in the harshest of conditions, my father never failed to ask about my studies. Whether through letters, phone calls, or rare moments together, he always discussed my future with my mother. He believed that knowledge was the greatest weapon, and he wanted me to wield it with confidence.

"Study well," he would say. "No matter where I am, I will always be proud of you."

Those words meant everything to me. They were my motivation, my strength, and my guiding light. I knew that no matter how far he was, his love surrounded me like an invisible shield.

I was truly a proud child of my proud parents. Their sacrifices, their strength, and their unwavering love shaped me into the person I was becoming. And though the distance between us often felt unbearable, I found solace in knowing that my father wasn't just mine—he belonged to the nation. And for that, I would always hold my head high.

My Father, My Hero Summary

In this chapter, Myra reflects on her growing understanding of her father's life as a soldier in the Hindasia Army. She vividly recalls the pride she felt in his uniform, the gleam of his medals, and the sacrifices he made to serve his country. Through the tender act of reading his letters—each one a mix of love, duty, and harsh realities—she experiences both the warmth of his encouragement and the pain of his absence. His rare homecomings and the stark realities of life at the unforgiving Snow Frontier, where he faced relentless danger and harsh weather, paint a vivid picture of his courage and the weight of his responsibilities.

Alongside the physical hardships of military life, Myra learns about the deeper challenges of their homeland through one particularly impactful letter. In it, her father contrasts Highland's natural beauty and resilient people with its stark social and political contradictions.

Although still a child, Myra is stirred by his words, slowly beginning to understand that her home is a land of both hope and struggle. This realization, coupled with her mother's quiet strength and steadfast sacrifice, forms a lasting imprint on Myra, inspiring her to hold her head high and embrace the values of duty, resilience, and change.

7. The Challenges of Growing Up

Early next year

I was stepping into my thirteenth year, studying in 8th Standard. I was fortunate to still have Miss Nidhi as my class teacher, and I cherished her teaching, her leadership, and her love for students every single day at school. Nani and I had secured the first and second positions in the previous class, respectively.

Gradually, I developed a deeper understanding of life. As a young girl, I had never realized that I would have to go through various phases of growth and transformation. At just thirteen, I experienced the onset of changes that were both unfamiliar and unsettling. I can never forget the day I was taken to the hospital directly from school.

I had always sensed that growing up would be challenging, but nothing prepared me for that day when change knocked at my door.

My mother took me to Doctor Pema a couple of times. I was frightened, being in the hospital for the first time under such circumstances. I had so many questions in my mind—Why was this happening? What was I experiencing? How was I supposed to handle it?—yet I struggled to express them.

On my first visit to the hospital, Dr. Pema greeted me with a reassuring smile.

"Don't worry," she said. "This is completely natural for a girl."

I nodded, though my mind was still filled with uncertainty.

"Thank you, Doctor," I replied hesitantly, glancing at my mother.

"You're welcome, dear," she said warmly. "You're a good girl."

She then asked, "Where do you study?"

"I attend APS—Army Public School," I answered.

"And which class are you in?" she continued.

"I'm in 8th Standard."

"Great," she said, smiling even wider.

I observed her attentively and thought, "This is why she chose this profession—because being good isn't something everyone can manage, even when they try,"

Before concluding, she advised, "Please study well and be a good person."

I thanked her once again and admired the motherly kindness she radiated. She then turned to my mother and began a more in-depth discussion. My mother was counselled more than I was, receiving prescriptions and instructions on how to take care of me. Before leaving, my mother expressed her gratitude.

"Thank you. I will see you soon," she said.

"You're welcome," the doctor replied. "It is our primary duty to serve you."

"It's our pleasure," my mother added.

"And don't worry," the doctor reassured her once more.

I wished that every doctor was as kind and understanding as Dr. Pema Ongmu.

As we made our way home, my mother patiently explained how to take care of myself and how to use the prescribed medication when necessary. I listened carefully, feeling overwhelmed by the depth of her concern. I wished my father could have been there too—holding my right hand while my dear mother held my left. Was that even possible then? Maybe, maybe not.

I recalled similar moments from my childhood—perhaps up until I was in 6th Standard—when I had felt so safe and protected. But now, things were different. "I'm a grown-up girl now. Maybe I'm no longer a child," I thought to myself. Time had changed, the environment had changed, and my life was transitioning into a new phase.

Exactly twenty two days later, I sat on the beautiful porch of our house, reflecting on how quickly everything around me had changed. The trees, the sky, the world—they all seemed older, more mature, and undeniably more beautiful than ever before. Looking at them, I thought to myself, "How quickly time passes and transforms everything."

Indelible memories of the past flooded my mind. Some were joyful; some were entertaining, while others were emotional and even fearful—like dreams from another time. I felt a deep, solitary connection to them all. Running my hands over my head, I closed my eyes, then opened them, and closed them again.

For the next few months, I remained under Dr. Pema's guidance, following her instructions diligently.

Over time, I began to understand my body better, and I learned to navigate the changes with more confidence. My mother, in many ways, was my greatest medicine. Her support, care, and understanding helped me in ways no prescription ever could.

My father, on the other hand, was my hero, though he wasn't always around. Every time I missed him, I closed my eyes and felt his presence beside me.

Even then, just as I do now, I had an insatiable thirst for knowledge, books, and education. I wanted to become a teacher and make a difference in my students' lives. I dreamed of shaping young minds and contributing to society in meaningful ways. This dream had taken root ever since I met Miss Nidhi.

At APS, I had witnessed the struggles and triumphs of teachers first. For the best teachers, teaching was immensely rewarding. They had the power to ignite curiosity, foster growth, and inspire students to dream bigger. However, the profession also came with its fair share of challenges—unmotivated students, a lack of foundational education, overcrowded classrooms, and an overwhelming workload.

I saw some teachers struggle with students who exhibited unruly behaviour, sometimes even resorting to violence. As I grew older, I realized that such behaviour stemmed from a lack of true education.

"A true education should always mould a student towards the right path in life and never divert them away from it," I often thought.

In addition, many schools in remote areas lacked proper infrastructure, quality teaching staff, and administrative support. The reality of 21st century education was that opportunities were not equally distributed. The rich had access to the best resources, while the poor struggled to keep up.

Who was to blame? The government? The educational system or, the Society?

Despite these challenges, I never abandoned my aspiration to become a teacher. Teaching was the only profession that could truly transform lives, and I wanted to be a part of that change.

Perhaps my motivation stemmed from the extraordinary education I received at APS. Just one year with Miss Sharma had changed my aspirations and broadened my perspective on education. She wasn't only an inspiration to students but also to her fellow teachers. She had a rare ability to instil positive values and transform struggling students into successful ones.

As an English teacher, she had numerous responsibilities—developing students' language skills, fostering creativity, and encouraging them to express themselves confidently. She introduced us to 'learning by doing'—a method that involved role-playing, extempore speeches, and practical engagement rather than rote memorization.

The Challenges of Growing Up Summary

As Myra steps into her teenage years, she begins to experience profound emotional and physical changes that leave her feeling uncertain and overwhelmed. Fortunately, she finds support in her understanding teachers and her mother, who takes her to Dr. Pema Ongmu for guidance. The doctor's warmth and reassurance help ease her fears, and over time, she learns to navigate this phase with more confidence.

Despite these personal transformations, her passion for education remains unwavering. Inspired by her teacher, especially Miss Nidhi Sharma, she aspires to become a teacher herself and reflects on the challenges in the education system—inequality, lack of resources, and the struggles of both students and teachers. Yet, she remains determined to make a difference, believing that true education has the power to shape lives.

8. The Legacy of Miss Nidhi

Miss Sharma was the best teacher I had ever known. Her presence in my life was like a beacon of light, guiding me through the maze of adolescence and shaping my dreams in ways I could never have imagined. I even started praying that I would one day stand in her place, inspiring young minds just as she had inspired mine. But as someone once said, "Don't try to copy anyone. If you do, you will end up becoming no one."

Still, I wanted to follow in her footsteps. She was everything I aspired to be—friendly, confident, and highly knowledgeable. She had a great sense of humour, excellent communication skills, and, above all, kindness in her heart. Her presence was a comfort, her words a source of wisdom. Each lesson she delivered wasn't just a subject but a journey into a new world. Her passion for teaching was contagious, filling our young minds with curiosity and an insatiable hunger for learning. I had built a strong bond with her over just one year or so, yet it felt like she had been a part of my life forever. I wished that one year could extend into a decade, or even longer.

My friends—Nani and others—felt the same way. Miss Sharma was more than just a teacher; she was a guiding light, someone who shaped not only our knowledge but our very personalities. She taught us discipline, kindness, and the importance of perseverance. She made learning feel less like a task and more like a privilege. Her classroom was a sanctuary, a place where we felt safe to express ourselves, to make mistakes, and to grow.

I once told Nani that Miss Sharma's name would be etched in everyone's memory. Little did I know that one day, I would turn on my laptop to write about her legacy. And little did I know that time would change everything, including my greatest inspiration's departure in pursuit of better opportunities. The thought of her possible departure filled me with a sense of loss, but I knew her impact would remain with me forever.

I remember one day, it was a cold winter morning at APS, and the students huddled inside their classroom, their breaths visible in the chilly air. The warmth of Miss Nidhi Sharma's voice was enough to keep us engaged, her words carrying the power to dissolve the cold creeping into our fingers and toes. She stood in front of the class, holding a worn-out book of literature. Her eyes gleamed with the passion she had for literature, and I, sitting in the second row, leaned forward, captivated.

"Literature is not just about words," Miss Nidhi began, her voice carrying the weight of experience and passion. "It is about life itself. The joys, the sorrows, the struggles—it teaches us to understand ourselves and the world better." She paused, looking at the young faces in front of her. "Who among you wants to write one day?"

A few hands hesitantly went up, but I did not raise mine. I had always loved writing, scribbling thoughts in my notebook, but I never thought it could mean something beyond personal expression. Writing was my secret, a way to make sense of the world and my place in it. It was my refuge, my sanctuary, but I never imagined it could be anything more.

Miss Nidhi smiled knowingly. "Sometimes, the ones who don't raise their hands are the ones who will write the most powerful stories."

Her words lingered in the air, and I felt a strange flutter in my chest. Could she see something in me that I couldn't see in myself? The thought both excited and terrified me.

That day, I read aloud a passage from *Where Life is Without Learning*. The words echoed through the room, as if they carried a message meant just for me.

Where life is without learning...

The words struck something deep within me. Until that moment, I had never thought of writing as a way to break free, to question, to dream beyond the boundaries of my own world. It had been nothing more than a personal escape, a secret between my notebook and me. But as I read those lines, something shifted. Writing was more than just an escape—it was a voice, a force, a path to something greater.

As the class ended, Miss Nidhi walked past my desk and gently placed the book in front of me. "You have a mind full of stories, Myra. Don't be afraid to let them out."

I looked up at her, surprised, but she had already turned to the next student. I held the book in my hands, running my fingers over its pages, feeling a strange mix of excitement and nervousness. Her words echoed in my mind, and I wondered if she truly believed in me or if she was simply encouraging me, as she did with all her students.

That evening, I sat by my window, the book open on my lap. The sun dipped below the Highland hills, bathing the town in a golden glow. The world outside was quiet, except for the occasional chirping of birds and the distant hum of life. I picked up my pen and, for the first time, I did not just write—I felt as though I was speaking to the world. My words were no longer just silent thoughts on paper; they were alive, breathing, waiting to be heard.

I wrote about my dreams, my fears, and the lessons Miss Nidhi had taught me. I wrote about the cold winter mornings at APS, the warmth of her voice, and the way she made us believe in ourselves. I wrote about the bond we shared, the moments of laughter and learning, and the impact she had on my life. And as I wrote, I realized that Miss Nidhi had given me more than just knowledge—she had given me a voice.

Years later, as I stood before my own students, I carried Miss Nidhi's legacy in my heart. Her words, her kindness, and her passion for teaching had shaped me in ways I could never fully express. And as I looked at the young faces in front of me, I hoped to inspire them just as she had inspired me. For in her, I had found not just a teacher, but a guiding light—a light that would forever illuminate my path.

The Legacy of Miss Nidhi Summary

Miss Nidhi Sharma, Myra's beloved teacher, leaves an indelible mark on her life with her kindness, wisdom, and passion for teaching. Through her lessons, Miss Nidhi inspires the protagonist to see writing not just as a personal escape but as a powerful voice to connect with the world. A poignant moment in class, where Miss Nidhi encourages her to share her stories, becomes a turning point in the Myra's life.

Years later, as a teacher herself, the Myra carries forward Miss Nidhi's legacy, striving to inspire her students just as she was once inspired. The chapter beautifully captures the enduring impact of a great teacher and the transformative power of education.

The bond between Myra and Miss Nidhi is portrayed with warmth and nostalgia, highlighting how a single year of mentorship can shape a lifetime. Miss Nidhi's possible departure for better opportunities leaves a void, but her teachings continue to guide the protagonist, reminding her of the importance of kindness, perseverance, and the courage to dream. The chapter is a heartfelt tribute to the profound influence teachers can have, not just on academic growth but on the very essence of who we become.

9. A Teacher Who Never Left (A Farewell to Remember)

In 2004, later that year, Miss Sharma had to leave, just like every other teacher before her. Yes, she had to leave APS. She had to leave us. It felt as though she was leaving forever for another planet. Everything was set for her departure, and the day had finally arrived. It was a bitter moment, like a real nightmare for all of us. But for me, it was even harder—I was the closest student to her. Despair filled the air as we looked at one another, memories flooding our minds. Her introduction to APS felt like it had happened just yesterday. But it hadn't.

As always, in the evening assembly, we stood facing our teachers, especially our favourite ones. However, this assembly was different. The atmosphere was heavy, the moment unforgettable. It was a life-changing experience, one that could either make or break us in desperation.

"Respected teachers and my dear students!" Ma'am Rashi began her farewell speech.

"We all know that our most impactful teacher, Miss Nidhi Sharma, is bidding us farewell. This is all for her better opportunities. We are here to say goodbye to a wonderful teacher who has greatly influenced us. I am here to thank her for everything she has done to transform our school environment and, more importantly, to transform you—the students. Our school will never forget her selfless attitude and contributions to this temple of knowledge. We owe her so much in so many ways."

A pin-drop silence filled the assembly ground. Every student was looking at Miss Sharma, and so was I—but in complete despair. I could read her thoughts from where I stood. I did not know who all were looking at whom, but my unblinking eyes remained fixed on her. Honestly, I had never imagined this moment, not even in my worst nightmares—at least not in the next couple of years. But here it was, arriving without warning.

"I hope you never leave the teaching profession in the future," Ma'am Rashi Roy continued, looking at her. Miss Sharma nodded and smiled, though I could see the pain hidden behind it. Smiling in a moment like that must have been one of the hardest things to do. But she did it.

Ma'am went on:

"You have made our school proud and left an unforgettable mark. On behalf of all the teaching staffs, parents, students, and most importantly, this institution, I thank you from the bottom of my heart. Even though you are leaving today, your name will always be remembered as one of the most inspiring personalities in our school's history."

"Highland will remember her," I thought with my misty eyes.

I ran my hands through my hair and glanced at Nani. She was speechless, and so was I. I looked around, everyone seemed equally awed. Closing my eyes, I listened to the principal's speech for a few minutes before opening them again.

"And I must tell you, Miss Sharma—you made a difference."

"Thank you."

"Thank you very much…" Ma'am Principal concluded.

Now, Madam Rashi turned to Miss Nidhi Sharma, who stood quietly beside her, her eyes glistening with unshed tears. Placing a gentle hand on Miss Nidhi's shoulder, Madam Rashi spoke softly, her voice carrying across the silent ground.

"Miss Nidhi, before we let you go, we cannot let this moment pass without hearing a few words from you. You have been more than a teacher to these children—you have been their guide, their friend, and their inspiration. Please, share your thoughts with us. Let us hear your voice one last time."

The students erupted into applause, their claps echoing like a thunderous plea. Miss Nidhi hesitated, her hands clasped tightly in front of her. She looked out at the sea of faces—students she had taught, laughed with, and cared for over the past year. Her gaze lingered on me, as I stood in the front row, tears streaming down my face.

Taking a deep breath, Miss Nidhi stepped forward. The applause faded into a silence so profound that even the wind seemed to hold its breath. She looked at Madam Rashi, then at the students, her voice soft but steady as she began to speak.

"Thank you, Madam Rashi, for your kind words," she said.

"And my dear students," she continued.

"Today, as I stand here, my heart is heavy, yet filled with so much love and gratitude. APS has been more than just a school to me—it has been a home, and all of you have been my family. Teaching you has been one of the greatest joys of my life. Every lesson, every smile, and even every challenge we faced together has left an indelible mark on my soul.

I may be leaving APS, but please know that a part of me will always remain here with you. Each of you has taught me as much as I hope I've taught you—about resilience, curiosity, and the beauty of growing together. Remember, education is not just about books and exams; it's about discovering who you are and daring to dream big. Carry that spirit with you always.

As I say goodbye, I want you to know that I believe in each one of you. You have the power to achieve greatness, to make a difference, and to shine brightly in this world. Thank you for letting me be a small part of your journey. Keep learning, keep growing, and never forget how much you are loved. This is not the end—it's just the beginning of the incredible stories you will write.

Thank you, APS. Thank you, my dear students. I will carry you all in my heart, always."

She paused, wiping a tear, and smiled through her emotions.

"Goodbye, and may your future be as bright as your spirit."

The assembly erupted in applause, tears, and heartfelt emotions all over. It lasted for more than a couple of minutes, echoing across the assembly ground. Even in her last moments at APS, Miss Sharma's love and kindness for her students shone through her farewell speech.

The unpredictable weather of the Himalayas, often wild and untamed, seemed to mirror the emotions of the day. Perhaps even nature was mourning the departure of Miss Nidhi. After the assembly, my beloved teacher gave all of us her best wishes. I was weeping bitterly over her departure, silently questioning the almighty as to why she had to leave. It was a bittersweet moment for me—while I wished her the best of luck, I couldn't shake the sorrow of saying goodbye. I glanced at Nani, who stood beside me, also weeping silently. Her tears were like a brook, while mine felt like a river.

A couple of drops of tears drifted down Miss Sharma's face. I couldn't help myself. I could see how genuine they were! She walked up to me, knowing I was the one who was feeling the most pain over her leaving, and gently consoled me. She comforted everyone, especially two of us, trying to convince us—and perhaps herself—that everything would be alright. But her tears betrayed her words. In that moment, I realized: 'The mind may pretend, but tears always tell the truth.'

"Don't cry, everything will be alright," she said, though we all knew how difficult this moment was.

"Thank you, Miss," I managed to say, nodding my head.

She looked at Nani, who nodded as well, her red-rimmed eyes brimming with sorrow.

"Don't worry," Miss Sharma continued, wiping her own tears. "You are grown up now, and you can't cry like little children." She smiled, and we smiled too—through our sniffles and heavy hearts.

"Study well and good luck with your future studies."

"Yes, Miss…" I whispered, barely able to form words. I looked around; we were the only three left.

Then, she did something unexpected. All of a sudden, she removed her wristwatch and placed it on my hand. "This is for you. It will help you manage your time well. And all I know is—you will remember me forever."

As soon as she gave me the watch, I forgot my own reactions. I did not know whether to cry because she was leaving or smile because she had given me what felt like the greatest gift of my life at that moment.

I couldn't understand the meaning of separation from a loved one. All I knew was: "Love is a gift, and it binds us no matter where we live."

Nani and I couldn't stop our sniffles, though we tried. Miss Sharma hugged us like a mother and embraced us tightly. Then she gave us a genuine, broad smile—a final farewell. It was the kind of smile only someone who truly loved could give at such a moment.

"How can she smile at this moment?" I wondered. Maybe she loved us that much. As we moved away with heavy hearts, we waved at each other and I turned back one last time. And then, she was gone.

On the way home, I reminisced about the day she entered my life—the day she introduced herself to us, the day we were asked to introduce ourselves, the day I first noticed her belongings, her beauty, and her kindness. It hadn't been many years, just about 15 months. But in that single year or so, we had built a bond that went beyond the usual student-teacher relationship.

She had become my mother at my second home, my true friend who understood the meaning of friendship, education, life, and support. She had treated us to lunch, cakes, sweets, and chocolates on so many occasions. Every single day over the past 400 days or so had been a new experience filled with learning, fun, and memories.

During my early teenage years, she introduced me to the world of literature, life, and learning. From Shakespeare to Wordsworth, she opened up a world I loved to explore. She kindled my love for prose and poetry, teaching us poems and stories beyond our syllabus. She instilled in me a love for culture, traditions, knowledge, and humanity. She gave me a strong desire to explore the unexplored. I held a profound respect for this bond, beyond any other human relationship.

Years later, as I stood in my own classroom, teaching my students about the power of words, I realized—Miss Nidhi's lesson had never left me. It had shaped me into the person I had become.

Time had moved on, and so had Miss Sharma. She had left for a different city, a new school, a better opportunity. The corridors of APS felt emptier without her presence. Her absence was felt in every lesson, every classroom, every discussion that once carried her voice.

But she hadn't truly left.

Her teachings remained, imprinted in my heart and in the hearts of every student she had touched. She had taught us that education was more than just grades and exams—it was about discovering ourselves, finding our voice, and daring to dream.

Now, as I stood before my own students, I knew I had followed her footsteps, not by copying her, but by carrying forward the essence of what she had given me. I hoped that one day, just as I had written about her, one of my students would remember me the same way.

Because great teachers never really leave. They live on in the minds they have shaped, in the hearts they have touched, and in the dreams they have ignited.

A Teacher Who Never Left (A Farewell to Remember) Summary

This chapter recounts the emotional farewell of Miss Nidhi Sharma, a beloved English teacher at APS, whose departure leaves a profound void in the hearts of her students, especially the narrator, Myra. Through heartfelt speeches, tears, and cherished memories, the school bids goodbye to a teacher who transformed not only the academic environment but also the lives of her students. Miss Sharma's kindness, dedication, and passion for teaching made her more than just an educator—she was a mentor, a friend, and a guiding light.

Myra, who shared a special bond with Miss Sharma, struggles to come to terms with her departure. In a touching moment, Miss Sharma gifts her wristwatch to Myra, symbolizing the timeless nature of her lessons and their enduring connection. Her final words of encouragement and her genuine smile, despite her own pain, leave an indelible mark on the narrator's heart. The chapter captures the bittersweet essence of saying goodbye to someone who has profoundly shaped one's life.

Years later, the narrator, now a teacher herself, reflects on Miss Sharma's lasting influence. Her teachings about literature, life, and humanity continue to inspire, reminding the narrator that great teachers never truly leave. They live on in the minds they shape, the hearts they touch, and the dreams they ignite. This chapter is a tribute to the enduring legacy of a teacher who changed lives and left behind a love for learning that transcends time.

10. The Weight of Goodbye (Healing And Growth)

With all those memories, I reached home and tried to sit down and relax—but I couldn't. I wanted to talk to my mother and tell her, 'Miss Sharma has left for a better future.' But the words wouldn't come out. I was confused like never before.

The wall clock struck 5 pm.

"Where is the face wash, Mom?" I grumbled. "I need to wash my face."

I threw a tantrum at myself. My mother knew something was wrong. She tried her best to understand me, but I wasn't sure if I even understood myself.

"Here it is," she said, handing it to me. "What happened, Myra? Are you alright?"

"I don't know," I muttered, rubbing my eyes.

"Is something wrong?" she pressed, coming closer to me.

"Miss Sharma left APS today!"

"What?" she gasped. I knew she hadn't expected her to leave so soon either. She had been close to Miss Sharma too, just as I had.

"What did you just say?"

"That's true. She left."

She stared at me, mouth slightly open. She felt the pain too—I could see it in her eyes. My frustration was barely under control. I was helpless. I couldn't hide my emotions, nor could I do anything about them.

"Oh, God!" she sighed. "But don't worry, my dear."

She tapped my shoulder and held my hands, trying to console me. I felt some relief. Still, I kept weeping inside, and she could feel my sorrow.

"Someone will come in her place," she tried to assure me.

"Mom, but she was an impeccable teacher," I sniffled. "How can anybody replace her? She was everything to me."

"I know, Myra," she said softly. "And I'm sorry, dear…"

"You are my best daughter, and you understand things in the best way. Some teachers leave their indelible marks on students, just like Miss Sharma did on you and the rest of the students at APS. But in every profession, people leave and others join. We have to accept that reality."

"Yes, Mom," I whispered and hugged her. I felt connected to her in every way.

"You are more than anything else, Mom," I murmured. She ran her hands through my hair, and for the second time that evening, I felt a sense of relief.

She prepared tea and set biscuits on the table. But how could I eat? How could I drink tea or swallow anything at that moment?

"Myra, please have some," she urged. "It's just the way of life."

"I don't want it now," I said, looking away. The Himalayan layers were almost hidden in the darkness outside.

"Listen to me," Mom said. "You will also become a teacher one day. And you will have to follow the same path. This is the nature of life."

Something clicked in my mind.

"I love her so much," I said. "What will happen to me? What will happen to all of us from tomorrow?"

"I understand, Myra," she said gently. She fed me a couple of biscuits soaked in sweet tea, as though I was still a kid.

"A mother is a healer," I thought, managing a faint smile.

After that, I tried to read, but I couldn't. I opened my *English* book, then another book, then my homework—nothing made sense. I even tried helping my mom in the kitchen, but I was too restless.

I went to my room, screamed into my white pillow, slammed the door, and let out my tears in despair. My mother, my best friend, was the only one who truly understood what I was going through. As I slowly healed, I began to channel my feelings into my studies and dreams.

The next day, Nani and Madhu Aunt visited us, and together, we spoke about the life of teachers and their impacts – their sacrifices, constant journey from one place to another and their dedication to shaping young minds. The words our mothers comforted us, making us realize that while teachers may leave for better opportunities or any other undisclosed reasons, their lessons and love remain with us forever.

Gradually, I began to understand the reality of separation. I accepted it as a part of life, just like literature and culture. I realized that true education teaches us how to endure every phase of life. And though no teacher ever impacted me the way Miss Sharma did, I carried her lessons with me forever.

Days turned into weeks, weeks into months, and before I knew it, years had passed. Yet, Miss Sharma's influence remained deeply etched in my life. I successfully completed my 10th grade in 2007 with an aggregate of 90% and later achieved 95% in my 12th in 2009, securing the highest marks in English Literature. Perhaps it was the impact of Miss Sharma's passionate teaching, or maybe literature was always a part of my soul, waiting to be nurtured. Whatever the reason, I found myself drawn to every literary work I encountered, regardless of its origin or style. Each piece spoke to me in ways I had never imagined.

Society, however, had a different perception of literature. Parents typically pushed their children towards science, engineering, or other job-oriented fields, believing that arts, particularly literature, lacked practical value in the real world. The rise of Information and Communication Technology (ICT) and the digital revolution only reinforced this notion. The world was changing, work cultures were evolving, and lifestyles were transforming drastically. Literature, in the eyes of many, seemed an outdated pursuit.

But for me, literature was different—it was invaluable. I held onto this conviction firmly. My mother and Miss Sharma had instilled in me an unwavering love for literature, a love that only grew stronger with time. From the moment I was introduced to its boundless world, I knew

I wanted to place literature at the pinnacle of academic pursuits.

Initially, my father held the same belief as most parents—that I should pursue something more 'practical.' But with my mother's support, I convinced him of my passion. I explained how I wished to carve my own path, how literature could shape not just my future but also the world around me. Gradually, he relented, and his approval became one of the happiest moments of my life. After all, my happiness was theirs too.

I often pondered—did one really need to be an engineer, scientist, or politician to make a difference in society? I realized that literature itself had the power to change perspectives, to shape lives, and to inspire revolutions.

Throughout school, I actively participated in debates, engaging in thought-provoking discussions. Some of the topics included *'Parents' attendance in school meetings should be compulsory,' 'Democracy is the best form of government,' 'Sports should be included in the curriculum,'* and *'Students should be retained if they fail in any subject.'* But the debate that resonated with me the most was *'Science is better than Literature.'*

That debate became my forte, my battleground. Nani, my dearest friend, and I won countless debates together over the years, at the Secondary and Higher Secondary levels, respectively. Each victory reminded me of Miss Sharma, the mentor who had ignited my passion for literature. Those debates not only earned us recognition but also proved our intellectual mettle to parents, teachers, and the larger community.

Amidst all this, school life came with its own share of experiences. I received amusing, sometimes outright silly love proposals—letters slipped into my bag, shy confessions from boys I hardly spoke to, and even one from a short, kind-hearted classmate.

Though it seemed laughable, I understood that such things were natural at our age. Unlike me, Nani enjoyed the attention. At times, these distractions left me unsettled, but she always pulled me back, reminding me to stay focused. Her unwavering support made me cherish our friendship forever.

The Weight of Goodbye (Healing and Growth) Summary

After returning home from school, Myra is overwhelmed with grief and confusion over Miss Sharma's sudden departure from APS. Despite her everyday routine and her mother's gentle attempts to console her, the loss feels unbearable. In an emotional scene at home, amidst small domestic moments—grumbling about face wash and sharing tea—Myra's sorrow and inner turmoil come to the fore. Her conversation with her mother reveals the depth of her attachment to Miss Sharma, a teacher whose influence went beyond academics, making her an irreplaceable guiding light in Myra's life.

As time passes, Myra slowly begins to heal, channeling her emotional pain into her studies and dreams. Her academic journey becomes a tribute to Miss Sharma's legacy, leading her to excel in her exams and actively participate in school debates. Despite societal pressures favoring more "practical" fields, Myra's passion for literature, nurtured by both her mother and Miss Sharma, remains unwavering. The chapter closes with Myra reflecting on the lasting impact of her beloved teacher, recognizing that even in the midst of goodbye, her lessons continue to shape her future.

11. A New Beginning: Behind The Facade

June 2009, was a month that would forever remain vivid in my memory. At eighteen, I was stepping into a whole new world as I embarked on my journey to HGC—Highland Government College—for my admission. The institution stood five kilometres away from Evergreen Marg, the bustling capital of Highland. My home, Rani Village, lay another ten kilometres beyond the city. Commuting daily was a conscious decision—I did not want to leave my mother alone back home.

She had been my rock star, my guiding light, and the thought of being away from her for long hours felt unbearable. Secretly, I wished she could join me in college. How wonderful would it be to experience that journey together? How would society react? I could only imagine.

When we arrived at HGC, the imposing structure of the college greeted us. The campus was alive with the chatter of students and the rustling of leaves in the gentle breeze. My heart raced with a mix of excitement and nervousness as we approached the Admission Department and then principal's office. I greeted the principal with utmost respect, folding my hands in a traditional greeting. My mother did the same, her eyes filled with quiet pride. The principal, a bald yet youthful-looking man, scrutinized my documents before posing questions about my academic interests, family background, hobbies, and, most importantly, my choice of literature as a field of study.

Perhaps he wanted to steer me toward a more 'secure' career path. Perhaps he was concerned about my employability after graduation. His concerns were valid—Highland was struggling with unemployment, and literature wasn't a conventional choice. But I was determined. "I understand, sir," I responded with confidence. "But my heart lies in literature. I assure you, I won't remain unemployed. If nothing else, I will find a way to be self-employed or become a great storyteller."

My mother listened quietly, nodding in support. Her presence gave me strength, and I could feel her silent encouragement as I spoke. The principal exhaled deeply. He was perplexed, yet I could tell he admired my determination. He removed his glasses, set them on the table, rubbed his forehead, and ran his hand through his sparse hair—gestures of contemplation. He questioned me further, trying to gauge if my conviction was genuine. Eventually, he smiled and shook his head, as if surrendering to my unyielding passion.

"Alright, Myra," he finally said. "Congratulations!"

"Thank you, sir," I responded, unable to hide my excitement.

"You're welcome," he said, collecting my documents. "See you soon."

With my admission confirmed, a new day unfolded before us, filled with the promise of change and the simple joys of everyday life.

Mom and I exchanged glances. We had done it. My admission was confirmed. As we left the college, the sky was a perfect shade of blue, with no signs of rain. The world seemed to be celebrating with us. My mother, who always loved shopping, insisted we visit the market. The cleanliness of Evergreen Marg always fascinated me. The streets were lined with vibrant shops, their windows displaying everything from colorful fabrics to gleaming kitchenware. We did a bit of window shopping first, admiring the displays without buying anything. Then, we stepped into a store to pick up some vegetables.

Even while buying vegetables, she carried herself with grace. As my mother browsed the aisles, my eyes wandered to a small bookstand in the corner. There, I found a copy of *The Book of Endless Echoes* by Robinson Smith, originally published somewhere around 1994 in North America. I had heard so much about this book, and I couldn't resist picking it up.

"Your choice is always wonderful," my mother remarked, smiling as she saw the book in my hands.

"You always look beautiful, Mom," I replied, hugging the book to my chest.

"Thank you," she said, carrying some of our bags. Her smile was warm, and I felt a surge of love for her. She had always supported my love for literature, even when others doubted its practicality.

As we continued shopping, she surprised me with another book, insisting I take it. "Anything else?" she asked.

"Yes, Mom," I said in excitement. "This has already been a perfect day." I picked up yet another book, *The Notebook* by Nicholas Sparks

"And, now I want something," she teased, her eyes sparkling with mischief.

"What is it?" I asked, curious.

Without answering, she led me to a restaurant with a sign that read "*MOMO SPECIAL*." The aroma of steamed dumplings filled the air, and my stomach growled in anticipation. Sitting comfortably at a corner table, we browsed the menu. A polite, professional-looking waiter brought us warm water, and I felt a sense of contentment wash over me.

"Two plates of *MOMO*, please," I ordered, glancing at my mother for approval.

She nodded, drinking her water in quick gulps. The experience was surreal—college admission, shopping, books, and now our favourite food. The only thing missing was my father. His presence would have made the day truly complete. I wondered what he would have said if he were here. Would he have been proud of me? Would he have understood my choice of literature? I pushed the thought aside, focusing on the moment. Yet, he already was aware of how his daughter's story would unfold.

"Myra?" Mom's voice broke my thoughts. "What are you thinking?"

"Nothing," I replied, though my mind was a whirlwind of emotions.

She probably assumed I was distracted by the waiter, but I wasn't. Instead, I was lost in the beauty of the day, the joy of being with my mother, and the excitement of starting a new chapter in my life.

"This city is so clean," I remarked, changing the subject.

"That's why it's called Evergreen Marg," she said proudly. "It's a place where dreams come true."

As we ate, she picked up a newspaper, reading the headlines. My mother had always valued education. "Literature is life," she mused, "while science is perhaps the discovery of it."

I wholeheartedly agreed. Literature taught us to appreciate the world in all its forms. Science demanded facts, while literature celebrated imagination and emotions. Both had their place, but literature would always be my calling. It was through literature that I had found my voice, my passion, and my purpose.

As I glanced at the mirror across the room, I saw myself—more mature, more confident. The girl who had once struggled to express her feelings was now standing on the threshold of a new beginning. "You are a beautiful young girl," Mom said, catching my gaze. "And that's the truth."

"Thank you, Mom," I replied, feeling a blush creep up my cheeks.

Her love made me feel beautiful. And as we left the restaurant, she held my hand and whispered, "You are my greatest inspiration."

On the way to our sweet home, I talked to my father and Nani over the phone and informed them about the admission and my passion. They were so happy. They were so happy that we could sense it even over the phone.

It took us nearly thirty minutes to reach home by Taxi. My mother wanted to take a shower, while I longed to rest on my bed, hugging my favourite pillows. After a few moments of relaxation, I sat across the table, eager to dive into the novels I had brought with me.

The pages of *The Book of Endless Echoes* beckoned, promising a world of love, loss, and redemption. As I opened the book, I felt a sense of anticipation. This was more than just a story; it was a reflection of life itself.

But as I began to read, my mind wandered back to the events of the day. The Principal's sceptical yet admiring gaze, my mother's unwavering support, the bustling streets of Evergreen Marg, and the comforting aroma of *MOMO*—all of it felt like a dream. Yet, it was real. This was my life, my journey. And as I turned the pages of the book, I realized that this was just the beginning. There were so many stories yet to be written, so many dreams yet to be realized.

I glanced at my mother, who was now humming a tune as she prepared tea in the kitchen. Her presence was a constant source of strength, a reminder that I was never alone. No matter what challenges lay ahead, I knew I could face them with her by my side.

As the evening sun cast a golden glow through the window, I felt a sense of peace. This was my new beginning, a chapter filled with hope, dreams, and endless possibilities. And as I closed the book for the night, I knew that behind the façade of uncertainty and doubt, there was a world of beauty waiting to be discovered.

A New Beginning: Behind the Façade

Summary

June 2009 marked a pivotal moment in Myra's life as she and her mother visited HGC—Highland Government College—for her admission. Despite societal scepticism about her choice to pursue literature, Myra stood firm in her passion, supported by her mother's unwavering belief in her dreams. The principal, though initially doubtful, admired her determination and granted her admission.

The day continued with a joyful trip to Evergreen Marg, where Myra and her mother shopped, shared a meal, and bonded over their love for books. Myra's mother, her greatest inspiration, encouraged her to embrace this new chapter with confidence. As they returned home, Myra reflected on the beauty of the day and the exciting journey ahead, knowing that this was just the beginning of a future filled with hope, dreams, and endless possibilities.

12. Echoes of Despair

"You are my mother's gifts," I whispered, hugging both novels close to my chest and closing my eyes, feeling their comforting presence. Yet, as the comforting words of my novels faded into the background, a stark headline on the newspaper pulled me into a more unsettling reality.

Just then, my gaze fell upon the newspaper, *Nature Express*, lying on the table. My mother must have placed it there, though I had failed to notice it at *MOMO SPECIAL*. The bold headline caught my attention: *Two Farmers and a Young Man Commit Suicide in West Highland.*

I put the novel down, picked up the newspaper, and took a deep breath before reading further. The article detailed their ages, villages, and possible reasons for their tragic decisions.

"Mom must have seen this already," I thought, placing my right palm on my forehead. But she was probably singing in the bathroom, unaware of my growing distress. I shifted my hand under my chin, lost in thought.

They looked beautiful in the picture. Yet, I couldn't shake the feeling that they were thoughtless.

So many questions swirled in my mind. What could have driven them to take such an irreversible step? Why did they not think of their families, their communities? Why is Highland, a progressive state, facing such an alarming suicide crisis?

Highland had always been portrayed as the wealthiest and most advanced state in the country, frequently winning accolades on national and international platforms. Outsiders admired its achievements, and tourists flocked to explore its wonders. Yet, beneath this perfect facade, an undignified crisis loomed—one that only a few were willing to acknowledge.

When I say undignified, I mean an unnecessary and reckless act—an act of surrendering to despair rather than confronting life's challenges. Suicide, in my eyes, is the gravest crime one can commit against oneself. Life is meant to be lived, not discarded. We must find purpose, believe in our worth, and understand that the world needs us to make it a better place.

Determined to understand the broader crisis, I turned to the internet and various studies.

One study explained that the *suicidal thoughts arise when pain feels insurmountable. A person may believe their existence is meaningless or that the world would be better off without them. In such moments, death appears to be the only escape from suffering. But these thoughts are driven by negativity, not reality.*

Another article said –*There are ways to find relief without resorting to death. Support systems, therapy, and meaningful connections can bring joy, love, and the chance to explore life's unexplored paths. Instead of giving in, one must ask—why is this happening? Is it due to a failing political system, unemployment, lack of education, or social injustice?*

I delved deeper, reading about Highland's socio-economic conditions. Was the government failing in its responsibilities? Were people driven to despair by poverty, broken relationships, or betrayal? The statistics were alarming, and my thoughts spiralled further.

The human mind is incredibly powerful—it can lead us towards despair or towards hope. We need to raise our voices against injustice, demand accountability, and push for systemic changes. Democracy gives us the right to elect leaders who serve the people. If we choose wisely, policies will work in our favour, bringing peace, development, and prosperity.

Yet, I wasn't mature enough to fully grasp politics. My understanding remained limited, but the weight of these issues pressed heavily on me. My head began to throb. The newspaper lay on my lap. I put it aside and lay down, running my fingers through my hair, unable to escape thoughts of the lost farmers and the young man. Their stories haunted me.

A few moments later, my mother emerged, freshly bathed, and prepared tea. She placed a cup before me. "Here's your tea," she said kindly.

I nodded absently, staring into the distance.

"Thank you," I said, though my mind was elsewhere. I wanted to express my gratitude for her care and love, but the words wouldn't come.

"You know what, Mom?" I finally spoke. "Your daughter isn't a kid anymore. She can prepare tea for herself from now on. She can also do for her lovely family."

"Great," she said, nearly choking on her tea in surprise. A few drops spilled onto my clothes, and I had to change instantly.

"Sorry…" she said, laughing.

"I was serious, Mom."

"For me, no matter how old you grow, you will always be my child."

"I understand, Mom," I replied softly.

She returned to the kitchen, busy as always. I stared at the steaming cup on the table. It looked beautiful—just like my mother and morning nature of the Highland.

My mind drifted back to the newspaper.

If they were still alive, they could have sought for help, found jobs, received better healthcare.

But I am not in a position to change the system. I cannot create opportunities for them.

Who is responsible for a better education system? The government? Society? Us?

Anxiety gripped me. "Why don't we convince ourselves that we are born to make a difference?," I thought. "Why don't people see their own worth?"

I needed answers. Maybe my mother could help.

In the kitchen, I helped her prepare dinner. The fresh vegetables filled the air with their earthy aroma. I remained silent, lost in thought. My mother noticed my unusual quietness.

"Are you okay, Myra?" she asked with concern. "Are you unhappy with your decisions?"

I shrugged, unsure how to express my turmoil.

"Yes, Mom," I replied simply.

But she saw through me. "You are my best friend, Myra. I know something is bothering you."

I hesitated, then finally asked, "Mom, why do people end themselves?"

She froze, visibly shaken by my question. "What happened? Who ended whom? And who committed crime or suicide? Tell me, dear."

I quickly reassured her. "Mom, I just read the newspaper. Three people took their own lives. You must have seen it at *MOMO SPECIAL,* too."

She exhaled in relief. "Yes, I read it," she admitted, relaxing slightly. "It's been happening for years. Newspapers report it every other week or month."

I clenched my fists. "And that's exactly why I'm frustrated! Nobody helps the farmers, the unemployed, or the poor—not even the government."

She placed a comforting hand on my head. "Life is about endurance, Myra. Suicide or any other extreme step is never the answer. No matter how deep one's pain, solutions exist. Family, friends, professionals—help is always available."

She continued, "Taking one's life only leaves behind grief and regret. Governments may fail, but that doesn't mean we stop fighting. We must stand on our own, demand accountability, and work towards self-reliance. True independence is the beauty of life."

I saw her tears glisten in the dim kitchen light. I wiped them away, feeling guilty for upsetting her.

"I'm sorry, Mom," I whispered.

"You don't have to be," she said, embracing me. "You are growing up to be a thoughtful young woman now."

In that quiet moment of shared understanding, I realized that while the weight of sorrow might sometimes overwhelm us, hope—and the strength of those who care—always lights the way forward.

That night, we continued our daily routine, but something had changed. I had found clarity through my mother's wisdom.

"You are my world," I said, hugging her tightly before sitting down for dinner.

Echoes Of Despair
Summary

Myra finds comfort in her mother's gifts—two novels—until a newspaper headline catches her eye: *Two Farmers and a Young Man Commit Suicide in West Highland.* Shocked, she immerses herself in the article, questioning why such tragedies occur in a state celebrated for its progress and prosperity. As she contemplates the crisis, she wonders about the role of the government, societal pressures, and personal struggles that push individuals toward such irreversible decisions.

Seeking answers, Myra turns to research, discovering that suicidal thoughts often stem from overwhelming pain and hopelessness. She reads about the importance of support systems and wonders why people fail to recognize their own worth. Anxiety grips her as she realizes she cannot change the system alone. Troubled, she helps her mother in the kitchen, her silence betraying her inner turmoil.

Sensing Myra's distress, her mother gently prompts her to share her thoughts. Myra finally asks why people end their lives, leading to a heartfelt conversation. Her mother acknowledges the harsh realities of life but stresses that suicide is never the answer. She speaks of resilience, self-reliance, and the need to fight for change rather than surrender to despair.

Moved by her mother's wisdom, Myra finds clarity. She realizes that while she may not have all the answers, understanding and questioning these issues is the first step toward making a difference. As she embraces her mother, she feels a renewed sense of purpose, knowing that love, support, and determination can help navigate even the darkest moments.

13. A New Chapter, An Old Friend

One month later, as I stepped into my college life, my mother's words remained etched in my heart. Highland's crisp morning air filled me with excitement and determination. With my father's blessings and my mother's love, I knew I was ready to face the world.

And perhaps, in my own way, I could make a difference.

My excitement knew no bounds, hoping that day would change my life forever. The weather was perfect, one of the best days of the year. A gentle breeze flowed through the taxi window, playing with my hair. Perhaps the wind was enjoying itself, I thought with a smile.

The driver turned to me and asked, "Is it your first day in college?"

For a moment, I was taken aback and my mouth slightly open in surprise. I quickly regained my composure and responded, "Yes, it is."

I reminded myself not to engage in too much conversation. "If I talk more, he might take advantage of my friendliness," I thought.

A few moments later, he slowed down and said, "All the best!"

"Thank you..." I replied, nothing more.

As he drove off, I caught his smiling face in the rear-view mirror. I adjusted my hair and clips once more, whispering to myself, "I just love the mirror."

He smiled even more. "Had he heard me?" I wasn't sure.

I had no idea why he wished me luck so warmly. Was he just a kind person, or was there something more? Maybe he was young, well-off, well-educated, and looking for his dream girl. But that was just my wandering mind.

To be honest, he was the smartest taxi driver I had ever met. I enjoyed our brief conversation, though I suspected he might have seen me as someone who did not easily smile at strangers. I despised arrogance in people, yet here I was, probably appearing distant.

He slowed down occasionally, as if wanting to continue our talk. I understood why. It wasn't a new thing—young boys often liked talking to young girls.

"Perhaps I am a young woman," I thought. "And he is the best young man."

He glanced at me through the mirror and said, "My name is Kesav. I'm from West Highland, I drive here."

"I am Myra, from Rani Village, not far from here."

"Great… thanks for sharing," he said with a smile.

He seemed even happier now, speeding up a little. "Oh, he was waiting for my name," I realized. I found myself laughing inside, amused by his charm.

For a moment, I wondered: how could a taxi driver flirt with me? Was he really a taxi driver? Was he pretending to be one?

"What's wrong if I am a beautiful girl?" I thought. "What's wrong if I attract the opposite gender? It's natural."

I knew my upbringing as the daughter of a Hindasia Army officer had shaped me to handle situations wisely. So, I did not take it seriously. As we reached my college, he slowed down and waited for me to step out. "Thank you," I said, handing him the fare.

"You're most welcome," he replied, his eyes lingering on me rather than the money.

His blushed face suggested he had found something he had been looking for. Maybe he wanted to talk more, to know me better. In truth, he did not look like a taxi driver at all. "How can you be a taxi driver?" I wanted to ask, but I kept it for another day.

Leaving the taxi driver's friendly banter behind, I hurried into the lecture hall, still buzzing with the excitement of new encounters. Inside, I asked some lecturers for my classroom. They pointed to a notice board. "You're a bit late for class," one of them mentioned.

"And I hate being late," I muttered to myself.

I hurried to the board, scanning for my Literature class. The class hadn't started yet, so I took a seat. As I settled down, thoughts of the taxi driver returned—his neatly tucked shirt, sunglasses, well-trimmed hair, blushed cheeks, and that charming smile.

Meeting new people from different cities and backgrounds excited me. More than anything, I was curious. Making new friends, exploring different cultures—this was why I had looked forward to college.

I missed Nani that day. If only she had been here with me instead of in Dream City, far beyond the Highland, in another state, pursuing her nursing course. We had studied together for 15 years or so at APS. I wished she were here for the next three years, at least.

It had been nearly six years since I had last seen Miss Nidhi. I often wondered where she was, whether she was still inspiring young minds like she had inspired mine.

Life had moved on, and so had I. College was a new world for me — busier, louder, and full of unfamiliar faces. The days of neatly pressed, school uniforms and morning assemblies had faded into distant memories, replaced by hurried walks to lectures, piles of assignments, and the newfound independence of being a college student.

But fate has a way of bringing back the people who leave a mark on our lives.

It was just another day at College and the first for the class. I was running late for my literature class, balancing a few books in my arms, when I entered the lecture hall. The murmurs of students filled the air as they settled into their seats. I quickly found a spot near the window and exhaled, trying to compose myself before the professor arrived.

Then, the students stood in greetings as the door opened.

A woman walked in, poised and confident. She placed her books on the desk and turned toward us. My breath caught in my throat.

It was *her*. Yes, *her*!

Miss Nidhi! Professor Nidhi, now.

She looked almost the same, yet somehow different. Time had added a quiet wisdom to her features, but her eyes—those kind, knowing eyes—hadn't changed. The same warmth, the same sharp intellect and wisdom.

I sat frozen in my seat, unable to believe it. My late childhood or adolescence' mentor, my inspiration, now stood before me—not as my school -teacher or a class teacher, but as my *college professor*.

"Good morning, class," she said, her voice steady and familiar. "I am Professor Nidhi Sharma, and I will be guiding you through this semester's journey in literature."

The room was silent, but my heart wasn't. It raced with a thousand emotions—joy, nostalgia, gratitude. The very woman who had once opened the doors of literature for me in APS was now here to do the same once again!

For a moment, she scanned the class, her eyes moving over each student. Then, her gaze landed on me.

She paused.

A flicker of recognition crossed her face, followed by a soft, knowing smile. She did not say anything, but she did not need to. That smile was enough.

She remembered.

And in that moment, I knew—some connections never fade. Some teachers are never truly left behind.

Professor Nidhi had found me again. Or maybe, I had found her.

And this time, I wasn't just her student. I was a young woman, ready to embrace everything she had yet to teach or guide me.

After the class settled, I gathered my courage and approached her quietly. "Miss Nidhi," I said softly, "I've missed you so much. You once opened the world of literature for me, and seeing you now fills my heart with joy and gratitude like never before in my life."

She looked at me with gentle warmth and replied, "Myra, you've grown into a remarkable young woman. I knew you would go far in life. When I see you, I see that spark of curiosity and determination that has always defined you. It's a reminder that the lessons we share continue to live on."

"Thank you, Miss Nidhi," I murmured. "Your guidance changed my life, and I promise to keep that flame burning forever."

I paused, feeling both vulnerable and empowered. "I want to thank you—for inspiring me to believe that literature can also change lives, including my own."

With a tender nod, she replied, "Remember, Myra, every story you read, every word you write, becomes a part of who you are. And some lessons, once learned, never fade away."

In that quiet moment of our conversation, I realized that some bonds grow stronger with time, transcending distance and years.

To my surprise, she had the same excitement, grace and love for literature.

When I introduced myself to the whole class, the boys clapped enthusiastically as though I was cracking some jokes there. More than Literature, they seemed excited about the introduction of especially, girls. "Boys will be boys," I thought and continued.

After the introduction, her eyes widened again in surprise. She walked closer to me, looked at my wristwatch, which was almost still the same even after five years or so.

She gently touched it and said, "We met again for a change," and gave me an old smile of APS.

I nodded, my eyes welling up. We were never in touch for the last almost six years for some reason, but we were here. The rest of the class had no idea what was happening between us. They simply stared.

Miss Sharma started her lecture: "What is literature? Why is it important? Why should we study it?"

"Literature is a collection of written words from a particular culture, language, or period in history…,"

I answered when she asked.

She smiled. "Well said."

I felt honoured. I knew she had influenced me somewhere along the way.

Some boys kept staring at her and the girls in the class. To their surprise, she wasn't married. But we ignored them. She continued, "Literature adds value to life. It spreads peace and happiness. It teaches us respect, harmony, and creativity."

She then quoted Charles Bukowski: "Without literature, life is hell."

That quote alone clarified why we were here—to see life through different perspectives, to grow.

As the day ended, I stepped outside. It was just 3 pm. I looked for a ride back home.

The day was full of rainfall and still drizzling lightly over Highland that afternoon, the mist weaving through the streets like an artist's unfinished strokes. I hurried out of the College gate, adjusting my bag over my shoulder. The semester had just begun, and I couldn't afford to be late for my first literature class, the next morning. I had to home on time that evening.

Just then, a taxi stopped right in front of me.

"Excuse me," I said to a young driver.

"Oh, hi…" he smiled.

"You go to Highland College, right?"

"Oh, yes. HGC."

I did not recognize him at first, but then it clicked. It was him—the taxi driver from the morning.

"I was actually waiting for you," he admitted, perhaps sensing my irritation.

"Oh…" I whispered. "But… what are you doing here?"

"I study here too," he said. "I'm a B.Com first-year student."

"Oh!" I was stunned. "Why did not you tell me in the morning?"

"I wanted to, but I thought I'd wait. And... you seemed a bit serious and hurried as well."

"Do I look serious?"

"Yes, but I like that. I mean, your personality."

I chuckled. "Thank you."

He opened the car door for me. I sat inside. His smile lingered. Maybe he had wanted me to sit in the front, but he did not say so.

He was a bit silent at first. I kept looking out of the window, pretending I did not notice him stealing glances at me. Then, as the taxi passed through the narrow lanes near our village, he finally spoke.

"I study here and drive taxis after class. It's a busy city—earning is possible."

"That's why you looked different now."

"Yes. It wouldn't look good for a student to drive in his uniform."

"Great!" I smiled.

As we drove, his red lips, sharp canine teeth, and warm smile almost distracted me. Then he added something unexpected.

"I'm the youngest son of Mr. Krishna Gurung, former Minister of Education, Government of Highland."

I knew many politicians had been caught in corruption cases. Was his father one of them?

"Oh, so you're a minister's son?" I asked, a bit sternly.

"Yes," he said simply.

On the way to home, I wanted to ask why he was working when his father had so much wealth. He could have easily lived his luxurious life if he wanted. But I saved that question for yet another day.

He talked about his family and their business across the state, the country, and even a few foreign lands. He shared his future plans enthusiastically. I wasn't particularly interested, but I still listened—he was enjoying himself, and perhaps it helped him to talk.

"I drive a taxi for my living and my further studies. I don't live with my family anymore because my father was involved in several ethical violations and corruption cases that tarnished our family's reputation beyond repair. When I questioned him, I was thrown out of the house—with just this taxi. I can't challenge him in any way; he has his grip on the government, the bureaucracy, and even the judiciary. But I have decided to stand on my own feet and live with dignity," Kesav said.

"You truly are 'Kesav,' just like your name suggests," I smiled, and he seemed to appreciate it.

"I may not be perfect, but I'll definitely try to live that way," he said.

A New Chapter, An Old Friend Summary

Myra steps into her new college life with excitement, carrying her parents' love and wisdom. On her way, she meets a taxi driver, Kesav, who surprises her with his charm and confidence. Though she remains reserved, their brief interaction leaves her amused and curious. Arriving at college, she quickly adapts to the new environment, eager to meet new people and embrace the academic journey.

In a shocking twist, Myra discovers that her literature professor is none other than Miss Nidhi, her childhood mentor who had once inspired her love for literature. Their unspoken recognition and silent exchange of emotions bring back fond memories, reaffirming Myra's passion for learning. As the lecture unfolds, Myra finds herself deeply engaged, realizing that some connections, no matter how distant, always find their way back.

On her way home, she unexpectedly encounters Kesav again, only to learn that he is not just a taxi driver but also a fellow college student and the son of a former minister. However, he has chosen to distance himself from his father's corrupt legacy, striving to build an honest life on his own. Impressed by his determination and integrity, Myra begins to see him in a new light, leaving room for an intriguing future connection.

14. The Unspoken Dilemmas or Bonds

The day had been a blur of new experiences, yet somehow, I found myself opening up to him. I spoke more about my family—about my father at the border and my mother at home. He seemed genuinely interested. When he learned I was from an army background, he asked a few more questions, though I could tell he had many. I answered them honestly. Yet, I did not ask him a single thing about his family—not out of arrogance or pride, but maybe because some instincts warned me that knowing too much too soon could complicate things.

I was raised to be brave, to fight for a better life, and to never be swayed by sugar-coated words. I don't mean to say he was trying to impress me for no reason, but he had a presence about him. Honest and self-disciplined—that's what I liked most about man. He spoke with sincerity. I knew he wanted to continue our conversation, perhaps even build a connection with me, and I understood that way.

At the taxi point, I asked him to stop. As I reached for my wallet inside the purse, he flatly refused to take the fare. Embarrassed for the second time that day, I hesitated—but I realized that money had no value in love or friendship. The only problem was that our relationship had no name yet.

I thanked him sincerely. "Can I wait for you here again?" he asked.

"And that is tomorrow," I thought. Without realizing it, I blushed, I smiled.

I did not want to refuse—not in the name of friendship. After all, we were going to the same college. "Sure," I said, knowing that my smile was what he sought as a sign of approval. His own smile, so charming and sincere, only enhanced his handsomeness.

"Thanks," he said, checking his seatbelt.

"See you tomorrow then," I said, stepping back.

As I walked home, the events of the day replayed in my mind—new faces, unexpected moments, and the lingering warmth of an unspoken bond. *Wow! What a day at college!*

"He's impressive. He's a positive young man. He's really handsome in his own unique way," I thought, shaking my head with beautiful black hair.

After walking for nearly five minutes, I reached home. The queen of our garden—my mother—stood in the distance, watering the flowers, her favourite pastime. Hundreds of blooms filled the air with their fragrance, making our sweet home even more beautiful.

The sweet scent of blooming jasmine was almost everywhere as I watched her. "She loves the garden as much as I do," I thought, stepping closer. She smiled with curiosity, I knew.

I changed my clothes and wanted to help her, perhaps with watering or cleaning. She was deeply involved in community cleaning projects and had participated in the 'Clean Highland' initiatives more than a couple of times.

She looked at me. "How was your first day, Myra?" she asked, setting the watering can down. She seemed tired.

"It was one of the best days of my life, Mom," I said, taking the can from her and tending to the garden.

"Wow! That's great!"

"Perhaps the best experience of my life."

"Great," she said again, "that's wonderful to hear."

I looked at her—her happiness was unmatched.

"I know you'll love it even more as time goes on," she added.

"I hope so, Mom. I learned so much in just one day. But maybe I also met someone I shouldn't have. I don't want to fall in love. And you know, Mom? I hate politicians more than I hate politics."

"What happened?" Her smile faded for a moment. "Oh, so does that mean you fell in love or met a politician?"

"I don't know, Mom. I think both, and maybe more."

"Wow! A surprise on the very first day of college, isn't it?"

"But," I clarified, "just the son."

"That shouldn't be a problem. Just stay away from politics," she advised, knowing my frustration with the corrupt system.

"Why shouldn't there be a problem when everything is messed up by these people?" I thought, remembering the stories my father used to tell about the false promises politicians made to soldiers, the way they used them as pawns in their grand speeches.

Every day, politicians were on TV, in newspapers, and on social media. They spoke of progress—reducing poverty, creating jobs, improving education—but in reality, nothing changed. Some leaders were good, but the majority were manipulative demagogues. They made empty promises, won elections, and delivered nothing.

Sometimes, they even invaded people's personal lives just to gain public support, ignoring the fundamental right to privacy. This was the dirty game of politics. It was never for the poor. It was for the rich, the businessmen, the families and friends of those in power. The poor remained unheard—ignored at all levels.

"Thank God! My father serves in the army," I thought, gazing at the setting sun. The evening sky was beautiful, and we both loved it.

"Don't worry, things will get better," my mother reassured me. She knew I was upset.

I nodded. "I hope so, Mom."

We spent more time admiring the flowers. A little while later, I realized she hadn't had tea.

"Our tea moment is here," I said, placing the cups on the table.

"Great," she smiled. "Thank you, Myra."

I smiled back, knowing how much this little ritual meant to her.

"Mom, let me take a quick shower," I said and entered the bathroom.

As the water flowed, my mind drifted to Kesav—his smile in the morning, the ease in his voice, the way he looked at me before driving away. The taxi ride, the serene highway, Professor Sharma's introduction—everything replayed in my head like a scene from a film.

From the moment we met until he dropped me off, something about him lingered in my thoughts. Questions ran through my mind.

"He's a good young man," I thought. "He's smart. He seems intelligent too."

I opened the tap again, thinking of his smile—and accidentally swallowed some water. I felt stupid. "Maybe he wants to spend more time with me. Maybe he even wants to marry me. Am I at a marriageable age? Can I fulfil my dreams if I marry now? What about my literary aspirations, my career? He's kind, but his father is a corrupt politician—that's a crime against humanity."

I stood there, lost in thought, forgetting to shower for a few seconds.

I did not know why I was thinking this way—more about him than even Professor Sharma. Perhaps it was my age, or perhaps it was the right time to understand myself. Maybe he was drawn to me, and maybe I was drawn to him, too. My pretensions wouldn't work anymore. I had no clear answer—just confusion.

Maybe my mother held the key to my dilemma.

I finished my shower. When I stepped out, she was already at the table with my favourite book, and tea—reheated because I had taken too long. She was waiting.

"Waiting for me?" I asked, realizing I had missed our special moment.

"Of course," she said. "That isn't the same tea anymore." Perhaps she had completed a couple of chapters from, *The Notebook*.

"I'm sorry," I said, trying to bring back her smile.

She sighed. "What took you so long?"

I simply smiled but couldn't speak up a word. I could see the hint of desperation in her eyes—our tea time was sacred.

I had to make it up to her. She was my dearest mother, after all.

That day, probably, she had wanted to discuss something important or perhaps continue the same topic—politics—which I despised. Politics was never in our blood, but circumstances forced us to think about it constantly.

"Silence is gold," I reminded myself, offering only a small smile. I chose not to answer her question, nor did I want to reveal that I had been lost in silly thoughts while in the shower. That would sound even more foolish, I thought.

"Thank you, Mom," I said, wrapping my hands around the cup. It wasn't as hot as I preferred, a reminder of how long I had spent in the shower. My mother had already taken a couple of sips. She never lost her temper, even in the face of insults or injustices. Her patience was unwavering—she merely wanted to educate me from every perspective of life.

"My mother has the patience of a saint," I thought, taking a long sip. In my eyes, she was the modern-day female Gandhi of the world, with her wisdom and serene presence.

"Let's go to the porch," she suggested.

"Good idea," I agreed, helping her carry the small table.

The sun was gently lowering behind the hills. A flock of birds soared across the sky, perhaps for the last time that evening. Chirping sounds filled the air, harmonizing with the croaking of frogs from the nearby river. Nature felt close to us, calling us to immerse in its beauty. We weren't Robert Frost or William Wordsworth, but we could feel the poetry in our hearts.

"Enjoy them..." she said, placing an assortment of biscuits on the table.

"Sure," I replied, allowing myself to sink into the melodies of nature.

My mother's face softened into a smile. "Nature has a power," I mused, and as if on cue, I began sharing my experiences from college that day. When I mentioned Miss Sharma, now Professor Sharma at HGC, my mother's delight mirrored mine. She knew more about Miss Sharma's life than that of Professor's one, than I did and shared her insights with me.

Our tea moments were always filled with conversations—politics, father's life, literature, old Miss Nidhi Sharma, and even Kesav and his family backgrounds, the gentle taxi driver who had become a part of my daily routine.

That taxi ride became the first of many conversations—ones that would soon challenge my beliefs, test my emotions, and shape the course of my college life in ways I never imagined.

Over time, our paths kept crossing—at the library, in the canteen, during college events. Kesav had an easy charm about him, one that made me laugh even when I was drowning in assignments.

I remember, every time my mother and sat together, she spoke highly of the conversation she had with my father and his sacrifices and bravery. They had both become emotional while discussing my future—my education, my aspirations, my security in life.

"How serious my Mom is when she talks about education, profession, and politics!" I could imagine.

I could feel the depth of her love, her sacrifices, and her determination for my well-being. I listened intently, not wanting to interrupt. There was always so much to learn from her words.

As the tea moment came to an end, she would pause and again continue. I wished she would continue. I longed to absorb more of her wisdom. Her positivity, patience, humility, and unwavering belief in a better future made her remarkable.

"And, by the way," she would say, "Dad told me he misses you so much."

"I miss him too," I said, wishing he were there, sitting across the table, sharing stories of his life. My eyes welled up despite my best efforts to control my emotions.

A few days later in the evening overcome by nostalgia, I rushed to my room and pulled out a few old photographs from the Amirah. One stood out—a picture of my father in his smart Army uniform, standing tall, holding me just above his waistline. My mother stood beside him.

"An Army officer always looks stunning in uniform," I thought. I glanced at my mother, whose eyes drifted toward the sky. Tears threatened to spill, but she held them back.

"My mother is strong," I realized. "How difficult it must be - to be the wife of an Army man?"

She missed him deeply, just as I did. It had been nearly a year since he had last come home. That one photograph brought all our memories to life.

She walked over and wrapped her arms around me. "I miss your father. His duty at the border isn't easy, but his love for us makes me strong enough to live this life with you today."

"This is a mother's love," I thought, feeling it resonate deep within me.

"This photo was taken about fifteen or sixteen years ago," she said softly.

I was shocked.

"You were hardly six or seven then," she continued.

I nodded in understanding.

Although I had always known that my childhood photographs were carefully preserved, I had never realized how many of them held such deep emotions. Each one told a story, a chapter of our journey together.

"Life moves so quickly," she said, her voice wistful.

I understood exactly what she meant. I simply looked at her and thought, "You are right, Mom."

I wished I could be like her when I became a mother myself. I wished I could have her strength, her wisdom, her endless patience. And, more than anything, I wished she would always be there with me. Was it possible? Perhaps it was, and perhaps it wasn't.

For a few moments, we sat in complete silence. I thought of taking sip of my tea, but it had turned cold. I pushed the cup aside and turned to my mother.

"This was one of the best days of my life," I told her.

She smiled—a smile that never faded, even in the most challenging moments. That unwavering smile was my mother's strength.

By then, I had begun to grasp the essence of literature, and perhaps, even of life.

"Life has an end, and that is a universal truth," I thought. "Death is inevitable."

Sensing my silence, she said, "Let's go to the kitchen."

"Okay, Mom," I replied.

"We have a special dinner tonight," she added playfully.

I looked at her curiously. She winked.

"Oh? What is it, Mom?" I asked, quickly following her to the kitchen.

"You'll have to wait and see," she teased, winking once again.

I had no choice but to wait, but that was the best part of our everyday life—our routine, our moments, our love. Even as I cherished my mother's love and sacrifices, a new kind of bond was forming in my life—one that I never saw coming.

The Unspoken Dilemmas or Bonds Summary

Myra's first day of college brings unexpected encounters and deep reflections. She meets Kesav, a charming yet sincere young man, whose presence lingers in her thoughts. Though she enjoys their conversation, she remains cautious, especially upon learning about his political background. Despite her hesitation, she agrees to meet him again, marking the beginning of an undefined relationship.

Back home, Myra shares her day with her mother while tending to their beloved garden. Their tea-time ritual strengthens their bond as they discuss politics, life, and the day's events. Myra wrestles with her emotions, torn between attraction and her strong disdain for corrupt politicians.

As the day ends, she finds solace in nature and conversation with her mother. Yet, thoughts of Kesav persist, making her question her own heart. Though she remains unsure, their paths seem destined to intertwine, setting the stage for something more.

15. Kesav and Myra: A Story Unfolding

One evening, after a long group discussion at the library, Kesav walked toward me. As we stood there, he looked at me and said, "You know, I never believed in fate. But after that first taxi ride, I might reconsider."

I laughed, shaking my head. "So you think we were meant to meet?"

"I don't know," he said, smiling. "But I'm glad we did."

And from that moment, I knew—this was just the beginning.

Thus began my journey at HGC—meeting Kesav, developing a friendship, and gradually understanding life beyond textbooks. He drove me to college for three years, and whenever he had extra time, he would take on passengers in the early mornings and evenings. Through every ride, every conversation, he became a comforting presence in my college life.

During my years at HGC, I was honoured with titles such as "Student of the Year," "Best Student," "Best Literary Champion" and even "Outstanding Literary Achiever" multiple times. Kesav, though an excellent student, never received any awards. Time passed, friendships grew, and I gained not just literary knowledge but also a deeper understanding of life.

As the years at HGC unfolded, my friendship with Kesav deepened in ways I had never anticipated. By then, I had started already calling him 'Kesu' and he loved it like never before in his entire life. What had started as shared taxi rides and casual conversations soon became something more—a bond built on understanding, respect, and unspoken emotions and that was the truth.

Kesu, despite being from a well-off family, never carried the arrogance of privilege or of anything. He worked tirelessly, waking up before dawn to drive his taxi, not just because he needed the money, but because he valued independence and the dignity of labour. He believed that wealth should never define a person's worth. His humility and kindness set him apart.

In the final year of my graduation, one summer in the rainy evening, as I waited for him outside the library, I saw him give away his umbrella to an old man who was struggling in the downpour. He stood there, drenched, yet smiling, as if such acts were second nature to him. That was my Kesu—selfless, compassionate, and always placing others before himself.

Through endless discussions about literature, politics, and life's uncertainties, I found a companion who truly listened, who understood me beyond millions of words. I admired his quiet strength, his unwavering integrity, and the way he carried himself, not being carried away under any circumstances—not as a privileged son, but as a man determined to carve his own path.

It was his kindness and nature that first drew me in — the way he helped strangers, never hesitating to lend a hand to those in need. He treated everyone with respect, from the college janitors or the caretakers to the professors, never making distinctions based on their status. His love for literature matched mine, and we spent countless evenings discussing books, dreams, and life.

One evening, after a long study session at the library, Kesav and I walked back towards the taxi stand in comfortable silence. The streets were nearly empty, the soft glow of streetlights stretching our shadows along the pavement. The cold air carried the scent of damp earth from the afternoon rain.

I hugged my arms, shivering slightly. Without a word, Kesav took off his jacket and draped it over my shoulders.

"You should keep it on," I said, though I didn't really want to give it back. His warmth lingered on the fabric.

He shook his head. "I don't get cold easily."

We kept walking, neither of us in a hurry to part ways. A slight breeze ruffled his hair, and for the first time, I noticed a faint scar just above his left eyebrow. I had never seen it before.

"What happened there?" I asked, gently brushing my fingers near the mark before I could stop myself.

He hesitated and his usual easy-going expression faltered. "It's from when I was just about thirteen or fourteen," he said after a moment. "I got into a fight protecting my younger cousin."

I frowned. "A fight?"

"A group of older boys were bullying him. I stepped in and took a stone to the face for it," he said with a small chuckle, but there was something else in his eyes—a quiet weight that wasn't there before.

I stared at him, a strange warmth spreading in my chest. "You've always been like this, haven't you?"

"Like what?" he asked, tilting his head.

"Someone who puts others before himself."

He looked away for a second, as if unsure how to respond. "I don't think about it that way," he admitted. "I just... can't stand seeing someone helpless in any circumstances."

Without thinking, I reached for his hand. Just a light touch. Just enough to let him know I saw him—not just the confident, kind Kesav everyone knew then, but the one who carried unseen scars, both old and new.

He glanced down at our hands but didn't pull away. Instead, his fingers curled slightly, as if memorizing the moment.

The taxi stand was just ahead, but for a little while longer, neither of us moved.

Next week, in the evening, as we sat under the twilight sky, he simply said, "Life is uncertain, Myra, but with you, I find certainty."

His words echoed in my heart, they echoed in my soul, and perhaps echoed in the Highland, filling me with warmth and carried by the whispering winds over the hills, we called it home. In that moment, I felt an unshakable warmth, a treasure of life and a quiet promise of belonging.

I looked into his eyes—steady, kind, unwavering. They held the weight of unspoken vows, of dreams yet to unfold, of a love so gentle yet so strong. The world around us faded, and all that remained was the certainty that our paths were never meant to run parallel but to merge, forever intertwined.

The stars above shimmered, silent witnesses to our promise. And as the cool breeze wrapped around us, I knew—no matter where life would take us, no matter what storms we'd have to face, this love, this moment, would remain. That night, with a heart full of love and certainty of my own, I knew—our journey was meant to be one, and that is forever.

He took my hands in his, his touch warm despite the chill in the air. "I have loved you in every unspoken word, in every glance, in every heartbeat," he murmured. "And I will love you in all the days to come."

Tears welled in my eyes, but they weren't of sadness—they were of overwhelming joy. "I have known it too," I whispered, my voice steady with conviction. "No matter where we go, we go together."

Under the vast expanse of the night sky, we sealed our love—not with grand gestures, but with quiet certainty. A promise, unbreakable. A love, everlasting.

Kesav and Myra: A Story Unfolding Summary

Kesav and Myra's story unfolds as an unexpected yet profound connection, beginning with shared taxi rides and evolving into a deep, unspoken bond. Despite their different backgrounds, Kesav's humility and kindness captivate Myra, who finds in him a companion unlike any other.

Through years at HGC, their friendship flourishes over discussions of literature, politics, and life, with Myra admiring Kesav's quiet strength and selflessness. Moments of warmth and understanding gradually reveal a love neither of them had anticipated, yet it feels inevitable—woven into the fabric of their lives.

One evening, as they stand under the twilight sky, Kesav's words affirm what Myra already knows in her heart—that with him, she finds certainty amidst life's uncertainties. Their love, silent yet unwavering, is witnessed by the stars above, a promise sealed in time. In that moment, Myra realises that their journey is not one of parallel paths but of destinies intertwined, bound by a love that will endure through all of life's storms.

Myra and Kesav, finally under the vast expanse of the night sky, they sealed their love, not with grand gestures but with quiet certainty.

16. Voices of the Forgotten

Life wasn't just about love and stolen moments under the twilight sky. Even as my personal life found clarity and warmth, the reality of HGC remained unchanged. Beyond the moments of love and certainty, a different struggle loomed—one that defined my years at the college.

One evening, as Kesav and I sat on the steps outside the library, he sighed, running a hand through his damp hair. The day had been long, the protests louder than ever. "It's frustrating," he muttered. "We fight, we shout, and they still don't care."

I looked at him, thinking about how different our battles were—his struggle for dignity and independence, my fight for self-discovery, and now, the collective battle of every student at HGC. Love and literature had given me solace, but the world around us refused to stand still.

The institution that was meant to shape our futures was itself crumbling under the weight of negligence. HGC students faced persistent challenges: inadequate infrastructure, a shortage of faculty, and the unfulfilled promises of scholarships. The classrooms were overcrowded, suffocating in both a literal and intellectual sense.

The library, instead of being a haven for knowledge, was a graveyard of outdated books that no longer reflected the evolving academic curriculum. The Science and

Mathematics departments struggled with a dire lack of qualified teachers, forcing students to rely heavily on outdated notes and theoretical concepts. Laboratories were ill-equipped, reducing practical experiments to mere textbook descriptions.

Despite repeated appeals, the administration remained indifferent. The corridors echoed with students' grievances, their concerns dismissed as mere complaints. But frustration has a way of fermenting into something more potent. What began as whispered dissatisfaction soon evolved into a movement too loud to be ignored. Student leaders emerged, backed by determined peers, and pressure groups took form. The fight for a better education system escalated from classroom discussions to the streets.

Banners were raised, slogans reverberated through the campus, and protests became an integral part of our academic life. Marches to the various district offices were met with cold shrugs from authorities who saw us not as stakeholders in the nation's future, but as troublemakers.

Even when the media picked up our plight, exposing the grim reality of HGC, the response from the concerned authorities was sluggish and insincere. They gave vague assurances, but nothing ever changed.

It was during this turbulent time that I truly understood the power of collective resistance. HGC students refused to back down, and our voices grew stronger with each passing day. What had begun as a demand for improved facilities had transformed into something greater—a fight for justice, equality, and the right to a brighter future.

Yet, the deeper I delved into this struggle, the more I realized that HGC was merely a microcosm of the larger decay in our education system. The roots of the problem ran deeper than a single institution. The very foundation of our state's educational policies was flawed, plagued by corruption, favoritism, and systemic neglect.

Random corruption seeped into every aspect of governance, creating an environment where merit took a backseat to political connections. Nepotism dictated appointments, and opportunities were hoarded by those with influence. Jobs were scarce, yet the salaries of government officials—especially the people in power—continued to rise. Education, the supposed backbone of development, was reduced to a political tool, an agenda rather than a genuine effort to uplift society.

"The biggest corruption of teachers is making students pass without actual knowledge," I often thought. "A teacher's role isn't just to push students through exams but to equip them with the skills for life."

The newspapers painted a different picture. Articles boasted of increased government spending on education, celebrated literacy rates, and projected an illusion of progress. Yet, on the ground, we saw the reality—classrooms devoid of resources, teachers overburdened and underpaid, and students lost in an education system that prioritized numbers over true learning.

"Achieving targets and collecting certificates isn't the real meaning of education," I believed. "True education lies in wisdom, integrity, and the courage to seek the truth."

But would they ever understand? Would those in power ever see beyond their vested interests? I wasn't sure. Yet, I knew one thing: a nation cannot progress without a strong foundation in education, healthcare, and human resources.

Who was to blame? The students who were forced to accept a broken system? The teachers who lacked motivation in an environment that offered them little support? The administration that turned a blind eye to our struggles? The bureaucracies that thrived on inefficiency? Or the government, the ultimate decision-making body, which had the power to reform but chose apathy instead?

Policies could have been implemented more effectively. Greater financial investment could have strengthened education, prioritized technology, and enhanced healthcare. But none of these seemed to be a priority. Schools, colleges, and universities alone couldn't bring about the necessary change unless sound policies were designed and executed with commitment.

I wasn't alone in my frustration. Many of my peers shared the same concerns, the same sense of helplessness. We were young minds filled with potential, but instead of looking forward to a promising future, we found ourselves tangled in a web of uncertainty.

Looking back, I barely felt as if I had completed a degree from HGC. Instead, my memories were dominated by struggles, protests, and an education system that seemed more interested in maintaining its broken status quo than in empowering students.

My time at HGC had been about more than just academic lessons; it had been an education in resilience, in the power of collective action, and in the harsh realities of the world, we lived in.

Perhaps, amidst all this chaos, we had unknowingly become more educated than we ever realized. Not through textbooks or lectures, but through the fight for what was right.

Voices of the Forgotten Summary

As Myra finds clarity and warmth in her personal life, the reality of HGC remains unchanged. Sitting with Kesav outside the library after another exhausting day of protests, she realizes that while love has given her solace, the struggles at their college demand attention.

The institution, meant to shape their futures, is failing its students—overcrowded classrooms, outdated libraries, and a shortage of faculty plague their academic journey.

Despite repeated appeals, the administration remains indifferent, forcing students to take matters into their own hands. What starts as frustration quickly grows into a movement, as protests and demonstrations become part of their daily lives.

As Myra delves deeper into the fight for student rights, she realizes that HGC's struggles are just a reflection of the larger decay in the education system. Corruption, favoritism, and negligence seep into every aspect of governance, turning education into a political tool rather than a means for empowerment.

Nepotism dictates appointments, and those in power prioritize their own benefits over the future of students. Despite the government's claims of progress, the reality on the ground is starkly different—poor infrastructure, overworked teachers, and a generation of students left unprepared for real life.

Looking back, Myra feels as though she hasn't just earned a degree but a deeper education in resilience, collective action, and the harsh realities of the world. The protests and struggles at HGC may not have led to immediate change, but they have shaped her perspective on justice, truth, and the need for systemic reform. More than anything, she realizes that true education isn't just about exams and certificates—it's about wisdom, integrity, and the courage to fight for what is right.

17. A Teacher's Calling

Three Years Later

Three years had passed since our voices echoed through the corridors of HGC, demanding change – demanding change, for a change. While the protests had taught me the power of collective resistance, they had also ignited a deeper conviction in me—I didn't just want to challenge the system; I wanted to be part of its transformation. That's why, today, I sat across from my mother, ready to take the next step.

It was a beautiful evening. The golden sunlight filtered through the gaps between the leaves of two towering trees, casting a warm glow over the surroundings. Birds soared above the trees, their wings slicing through the sky in graceful arcs. The world seemed perfect in that moment.

"Mom," I called, watching her as she was engrossed in her book.

Her reading was my learning—a source of inspiration.

"It's tea time," I reminded her.

"Yes!" she exclaimed, without lifting her eyes from the pages. She was thoroughly immersed in her book, and I found joy in simply observing her. It was then that I noticed what she was reading—the very book we had bought three years ago from Evergreen Marg, on the day of my admission to HGC. Despite the passing years, the book looked as pristine as ever. No surprise there; we had always cherished our books dearly.

Over the past three years, we had developed a deeper understanding of literature, poetry, knowledge, and even politics. Our love for learning had only grown stronger. The only noticeable change was that my mother had gained a little weight, yet she was just as beautiful as ever.

Normally, she wouldn't speak while reading; she had a way of losing herself in the world of imagination. That was the magic of literature, and I still believed in its power.

"I want to talk about something important today," I said, placing her tea on the same old wooden table before sitting beside her.

She gently put down her book, picked up her cup, and took a small sip.

"Okay, Myra. What is it?" she asked, her voice calm.

"You should be relaxed now. College is over," she added with a smile.

"Yes, Mom," I said, "college is over, and that's why I want to live my dream."

She met my gaze knowingly. "And I know exactly what that is," she said, pinching my cheek affectionately. "You're not a little girl anymore, and I'm so proud of you."

Then she paused and added, "But do you think you will find a teaching job here, in this situation?"

"Honestly, I don't know, Mom," I admitted. "But I read in the newspaper that some teaching positions are vacant at BMSS. I thought I'd apply."

She suddenly flinched, her eyes widening. "BMSS? You mean the school run by Mr. D.D.?"

"Yes," I said, taking a sip from my cup.

She hesitated before asking, "Do you think you can make any difference there if you get the job? You should stand by your convictions."

I took a deep breath. "Mom, I believe I was born to make a difference."

She studied me for a moment before finishing her tea. As she placed the empty cup on the table, she reached for my hands and held them warmly.

"Myra, you have always aspired to be a teacher, and I have always supported your dream. You are now a young woman with a first-class degree in literature. You must do what you truly love, not just what you like."

"I love this profession, Mom," I said, resting my head on her lap like a child. She allowed it, and I cherished the moment.

The power of a mother's love can change everything in a child's life, I thought. She wasn't just my mother; she was my guiding light, the one who helped me see the world clearly even when I was lost in confusion. To me, she was the mother of the country itself.

She continued, "I love the way you are, and I admire your passion for teaching. But, Myra, I don't know if you can make a real difference at BMSS. There are many ways to bring change—in education, in society, in politics, and even in personal choices."

I wanted to say, "Not in politics, at least," but I held my tongue.

She went on, "BMSS is plagued with internal politics. Teachers are underpaid, but expected to deliver high-quality education. The hostellers live in poor conditions, and teachers are not treated with the respect they deserve. They talk about quality education, but they do little to implement it. As a result, students are not receiving the kind of education they are entitled to. Their future looks uncertain—a darkness looming on the other side of the same coin."

She sighed, then added, "The school was founded in 1990 by Sir DD, one of the most influential politicians of his time. BMSS once had a stellar reputation, and it is still affiliated with the central board, but now, it is run as a business rather than an educational institution.

Mr. D.D. makes all the decisions, and no one dares to question him. He claims to have multiple degrees from reputed universities, but no one has ever seen proof. He prioritizes money over quality, politics over education."

I was dumbstruck.

"How could an educational institution be run like a business?" I thought.

"Why is politics creeping into every sphere of Highland?"

I took a deep breath. "Then what should I do, Mom?" I asked, seeking her guidance.

She gently pressed my hands. "Maybe you should pursue a B.Ed. It will prepare you for teaching, and the government has made it mandatory for aspiring teachers."

B.Ed. and compulsory—the words were new to me.

"Another two years before I can teach? Another two more years before I can be a teacher?" I murmured.

"Most likely, yes," she said. "There are a few B.Ed. colleges in Evergreen Marg, a few in West Highland and a few in the East. We can visit them and find the best one for you."

Her words filled me with hope. I smiled, reassured. As she walked into the room, her phone rang. It was Daddy. I recognized his unique ringtone.

I sat there, deep in thought.

"Will I find a good B.Ed. college in Highland? What if I don't?"

But for now, I held onto one certainty—I had a path to follow.

For nearly three months, I kept checking with friends and relatives about the admission and selection procedures for B.Ed. programs all over the Highland. Nani, hadn't yet returned from Dream City. I wished she had. She had recently secured a job in the city, and everyone was right when they said, "She was in a job-oriented stream." I reached out to my friends, met with them, and discussed my aspirations, but most had little interest in teaching.

"We don't want to become teachers," some said. "Teaching isn't my cup of tea," others added dismissively.

I even called Kesav to talk about it, though I already knew he was merely interested. He had matured a lot and developed his passion for serving the nation over the years but was still driving the same taxi for his livelihood. Our bond had grown stronger, filled with love and mutual understanding. The past three years had been a journey of self-discovery for both of us, a realization that had touched us deeply.

I couldn't understand why my friends were so disinterested in pursuing a B.Ed. I wanted to know their reasons. Some told me, "Getting admission in B.Ed. programs is only for the rich, powerful and exceptionally talented families, or those who can pay bribes." That was yet another example of corruption—this time, in the name of education and humanities.

I recalled something I had read before: When there is corruption in education, society never progresses.

Each time I encountered such harsh realities, I felt an intense urge to change the system—to reform the way politicians functioned, to shift people's perspectives on education, and to transform the administration for better governance.

A Teacher's Calling
Summary

Three years after the student protests at HGC, Myra remains deeply committed to transforming the education system. As she sits with her mother on a peaceful evening, she shares her dream of becoming a teacher. However, her mother warns her about the harsh realities of BMSS, a once-reputed school now plagued by corruption and mismanagement under the control of a powerful politician, Mr. D.D.

Though Myra is eager to make a difference, she learns that pursuing a B.Ed. is now mandatory for teaching. Despite her initial hesitation about the additional two years of study, she finds hope in her mother's support and begins exploring admission opportunities.

Determined to follow her passion, Myra seeks advice from friends and family, only to discover that many see teaching as an undervalued profession dominated by political influence and bribery. Even Kesav, who has matured over the years, is only mildly interested in her journey.

The disillusionment of her peers strengthens Myra's resolve to fight for change. As she reflects on the corruption within the education sector, she realizes that true progress in society is impossible without integrity in learning. With a renewed sense of purpose, she prepares to take the next step toward her calling.

18. A Step Towards the Dream

The past few weeks had been filled with restless nights and countless thoughts about my future. Teaching had always been a dream, but now, as I stood at the threshold of making it a reality, I felt a mix of excitement and nervousness. I knew this journey wouldn't be easy—getting admission, financial concerns, and the competitive nature of the entrance exam loomed in my mind. But I also knew that this was my path, and I had to walk it with confidence.

With that in mind, my mother and I sat down to compile a list of B.Ed. colleges not just within the state but across the country as well. Nani, helped us even from the Dream City in the process. Mom, handed me the list, and I read through it carefully:

Evergreen Marg Government B.Ed. College (Estd.1980), Highland B.Ed. College (Estd.1985), Himalayan B.Ed. College (Estd. 1995), Kanchan City B.Ed. College (Estd. 2005), Serene Wood B.Ed. College (Estd. 2000)

"I would love to inquire at Evergreen Marg," I said, hoping it would be possible soon.

"Alright, let's give it a try," my mother agreed.

I nodded, feeling both excited and apprehensive. However, I did my best to hide my confusion. Among these institutions, only Evergreen Marg was a government college. The others were private, which meant higher tuition fees—something I wanted to avoid. My parents would not hesitate to send me to a private institution for the sake of my aspirations, but I wanted to be responsible and minimize the financial burden on my family.

I had often discussed my dreams with Kesav, who always listened patiently. He wasn't someone who openly shared his struggles, but I could sense that, like me, he was figuring out his own path. Perhaps that's why we understood each other so well—we both carried unspoken dreams, waiting for the right moment to unfold them.

That morning, I spoke with Kesav again. We discussed my plans in detail.

"Nowadays, the colleges perhaps have an online admission system," he informed me. "You don't need to visit in person. You can complete the entire process online if you want to sit for the entrance exam."

His words stayed with me, and at the right moment, they clicked in my mind.

In the evening, my mother and I sat across the table and turned on my brand-new laptop. It was a kind of birthday gift from my father. I had bought it recently with the money he had sent. I felt a wave of gratitude—I did not have to go around asking, "How do I operate a computer or use the internet?" At least I was familiar with MS Office and the internet, skills I had learned during leisure time in the college days and for now, that was enough.

I was quite happy, and Mom was equally excited as it was the first time we were doing something new like that on the laptop. On the official website of the college, I checked and found that the registration for the B.Ed. Entrance Exam was ongoing, and the last dates for payments, registration, and document submission were clearly mentioned. I got more excited.

I filled up the forms online with all the necessary scanned documents, photographs, and signatures. The payment was successfully processed, and I was the happiest young girl in the Highland on that day. It truly made my day. I informed my parents first, and Nani then Kesav and the friends about the successful registration. They were just as delighted as I was. From that day onwards, I started preparing for the entrance exam with complete dedication. I bought a few more books for the preparation from the market that boosted my confidence immensely.

One of Kesav's friends from HGC was also sitting for the entrance. He was wealthy and from a political background. However, he wasn't interested in teaching; his father had insisted he pursue this path, Kesav had told me, the previous week.

Exactly one month later, the day of the entrance exam arrived. I was confident yet a little nervous at the same time. I chose a simple yet formal dress, as appropriate attire was important for such an examination.

"All the best," Mom said, gently tapping my head. "This is the very first step toward your dream profession."

Earlier in the morning, Dad had wished me success over the phone. I also received a heartfelt wish from Kesav, a few more encouraging messages from friends, and warm wishes from my dear Nani and blessing from her mother, Madhu Aunt.

Their wishes and words filled me with warmth. My mother had always believed in me, and that day was no exception. She had shaped me into a good human being, and her blessings reassured me.

"And I know you can do well."

"Thank you, Mom," I said, hugging her in a bit of a hurry. "You are more like my elder sister and best friend," I thought, feeling an overwhelming sense of love.

"I'll see you in the evening, Mom," I said as I stepped out.

Kesu, had offered to drop me off, so he was already waiting on the point, the same highway—the national highway that had witnessed our bond grow over the past three years or so. We hadn't seen each other in about five months as he was out of town for some reason. As I approached, I noticed a few changes—his beard was longer, his hair slightly unkempt, and his taxi looked older. Yet, his presence was as familiar as ever.

"Hi," I greeted him. "Good morning!"

"Good morning," he responded in his usual lovely and friendly manner. I got in and relaxed as we adjusted our seatbelts, always mindful that "prevention is better than cure."

"Best of luck," he said with a smile, revealing his endearingly imperfect canine teeth that had always captivated me.

"Thank you," I said, blushing. "You haven't changed at all over the years."

"Still the same," I thought. "The same old Kesav."

"Probably yes," he replied as we started moving. Then, with a contemplative tone, he continued, "As you know I graduated from a well-recognized college, of the Highland six months back, but still I am not crazy about jobs, and a bit struggling to settle into my chosen profession. Yet, I love my job—driving. No matter what profession you choose, dignity in life is what truly matters. By the way, I admire your Dad's life and his sacrifice."

His voice softened. We had no marriage plans yet. How could we take a step like that easily? "Nobody wants a struggling father and a mother burdened by hardships. My father does not care about my future, but my mother does. I visit home only for my dear mother and a loving sister," he said with full of dreams.

"All mothers are the same," I thought quietly.

"Don't worry," I said reassuringly. "You're a master of driving. We'll lead a better life, and I have a faith in our future."

He glanced at me, and for a fleeting moment, he almost held my right hand—but he hesitated. Instead, he said, "Thanks for trusting me and our unspoken bond of love. We'll soon be together."

"You are different," he added, shaking his head. "You are so different in conviction and nature."

Maybe he wanted to confess something—to tell me that together we could build a future- a future that is a dream of every young woman and a man. I couldn't quite decipher his emotions at that moment.

"I am not," I said. "I owe you more than anyone else."

This time, he truly held my hand and said, "Please, don't ever say that. You are my friend, love and my inspiration in so many ways. You are beautiful—inside and out. I have never met anyone like you, nor can I ever imagine someone like you in my life. Every time I see you, my heart races, but I never tell you... because I can't tell you. Your beauty makes me nervous."

"I was right," I thought. "He wanted to tell me something."

The warmth of his touch sent an unfamiliar yet comforting sensation through me. I realized I had closed my eyes, and when I opened them, I saw a tall iron gate. The sign read: "*Evergreen Marg B.Ed. College.*"

I stepped out of the taxi, suddenly aware of something different about him that day—his look, his eyes, and his many more unspoken words. I felt them for the first time, though neither of us said a word there. Perhaps silence was the most honest expression at that moment.

I hurried towards the entrance reminding Kesav to pick me up in about three hours. He nodded, giving me a thumbs-up before driving away, likely intending to earn a little during those odd hours of the day.

I wasn't that late so I checked my roll number and found: *Roll No.:1143, Room No. 11, Row: 10.* The college campus was bustling with candidates. I scanned the crowd, wondering how many of them genuinely wanted to pursue teaching and how many were simply here due to parental pressure.

With a deep breath, I stepped into the examination hall, ready to take the first real step towards my dream.

The exam hall was crowded. Some of the students looked serious and others, unsure. A few boys loitered near the entrance, smoking and staring at the young girls. Discipline was lacking. Inside the hall, I noticed a group of students—long, unkempt hair, silver chains, torn jeans. One was even wearing home slippers.

A silence settled over the room as the invigilators entered.

Now, the test began.

The questions were intriguing—comprehension passages, general knowledge, current affairs, and computer-based questions. English was my strength, and I enjoyed every part of it.

During the exam, I noticed students scratching their heads, biting their pens or even nails, glancing around for answers. Some looked utterly lost. But I remained calm and focussed.

When it was over, I stepped outside the main Exit Point. Kesav was already there. This time, he wasn't smiling.

"How was your exam?" he asked.

"Great," I said. "Let's go, it's about to rain." I texted Mom and Nani immediately, coming out of the College gate.

It was all in the middle that great summer in Highland. Thunder rumbled, and dark clouds loomed. We stopped at *HIGHLAND MOMO CORNER*, about 5 Kms away from the college. Rain poured down heavily. Inside, we watched people dance in the rain, in the distance. I couldn't resist—I ran down outside and joined in.

"You'll fall sick," Kesav protested.

But I laughed and twirled under the rain. Eventually, he joined us.

Soaked, we returned to his taxi, a bit of shivering due to Highland's cool weather all throughout the year. He pulled off his jacket and wrapped it around me.

"You really love the rain," he said, chuckling. "You remind me of a peacock dancing."

I smiled. We smiled, we laughed together.

"And you'd make a great poet."

As he dropped me to the point, he declined my invitation to come along.

"I'm all wet," he said. "If I fall sick, who'll drive my taxi?"

We laughed again with all our hearts open.

I nodded, stepping out. He waved as he drove off.

Standing in the misty evening, I wondered, "What does a young, educated woman really want from a man like him?" The answer remained elusive, yet somehow, that day felt perfect.

As soon as I stepped into the house, I heard my mother's voice drifting from the kitchen, calm yet filled with emotion.

"Yes, she's absolutely fine here," she said, her tone carrying warmth and reassurance.

I knew instantly that she was speaking to my father. Lately, their conversations had revolved around his upcoming retirement, and today seemed no different. My heart swelled with excitement at the thought of his return. He had spent over two decades serving the Hindasia Army, and now, finally, he was coming home for good.

"Dad, I love you," I whispered to myself, feeling a wave of happiness over me.

Drenched from the sudden downpour that had caught me on the way home, I hurried to my room. I did not want my mother to see me soaked—she would worry unnecessarily. Slipping into dry clothes, I quickly took a shower, letting the warmth cleanse away the chill of the rain. By the time I stepped out, she was still engaged in conversation, her voice carrying through the hallway.

We were beyond thrilled knowing that in just a few weeks, he would be with us, waking up under the same roof, sharing meals, and laughing like we used to. He told us he missed us every single day, and we reassured him that we felt the same. The conversation ended with him wishing me luck for my results, and I could hear the pride in his voice even through the phone.

It wasn't officially tea time yet, but the moment felt right. I joined my mother in the kitchen, where she greeted me with a knowing smile. I eagerly shared every detail about my day—the exam, the laughter, the *impromptu* dance in the rain at Evergreen Marg. She listened with rapt attention, her eyes shining with pride.

"I'm certain you'll make it to the merit list," she said, her voice unwavering.

I nodded with the same confidence, the excitement bubbling in my chest. She gave me a look filled with love and said, "Your father is coming next month. He's already planned everything."

"Yes, Mom. That's the best news ever," I said, wrapping my arms around her. She held me tightly, as if sealing the moment forever.

"We will be a complete family now," she murmured, her voice thick with emotion.

I saw the unspoken years of longing in her eyes—the waiting, the resilience, the silent sacrifices she had made all these years.

"He has served the nation for over twenty years," she continued. "That is a remarkable achievement, and we are so proud of him."

"I can't wait to see him, Mom."

She sighed, her emotions surfacing. "Your father has earned respect, not just for himself, but for this family. I'm a proud woman, a proud wife, and most importantly, a proud mother—for I have a daughter like you. And now, nothing—not even fate—can separate us anymore."

I saw the wrinkles on her face, the silver strands in her hair, but none of them took away the radiance of her love. I reached out, wiping the tears from her eyes—and mine.

At that moment, I wished we could control life before it controlled us.

A Step Towards the Dream Summary

For weeks, Myra is restless, consumed by thoughts of her future. Becoming a teacher has always been her dream, but the journey ahead feels uncertain—securing admission, financial concerns, and the pressure of competition weigh heavily on her. With her mother's constant support and encouragement from Nani and Kesav, she meticulously shortlists colleges and finally applies to Evergreen Marg Government B.Ed. College.

The admission process is unfamiliar, but with determination, she successfully registers for the entrance exam. She dedicates herself to intense preparation, balancing excitement and anxiety as the exam day approaches. On the morning of the test, her parents, friends, and Kesav send their warm wishes, their belief in her strengthening her resolve.

Kesav, who has been away for months, drives her to the exam centre. Their conversation is filled with unspoken emotions—hints of a true love story waiting to unfold. His words about dignity and perseverance stay with her, giving her confidence. Inside the exam hall, she observes the contrast among candidates—some determined and others indifferent, and a few simply following their parents' wishes. The test is challenging, but she faces it with courage, knowing she has worked hard.

Afterward, she reunites with Kesav, and together they share a lighthearted moment in the rain—a rare escape from their worries. Returning home, she is met with unexpected joy—her father, a dedicated soldier who has served for over two decades, will soon retire and return home for good.

As she sits with her mother, sipping tea and sharing the events of the day, a deep sense of fulfillment washes over her. She is on the path to achieving her dream, her father is coming home, and despite life's uncertainties, love and support surround her. In that moment, she realizes that while life is unpredictable, it is also beautifully woven with hope, dreams, and the people who truly matter.

19. Ties That Endure

Exactly one year later:

"Good morning, Dad," I mumbled, rubbing my eyes, still half-asleep.

"Good morning, Myra," he responded, his voice warm. "Let's have tea."

At the mention of tea, my eyes fluttered open. "Okay, Dad," I said eagerly, pushing off the covers.

When I walked into the kitchen, my heart swelled at the sight before me. My father, a disciplined Army man, was helping my mother prepare breakfast, his movements precise yet gentle. It was a sight I had longed for, and now, it was real.

This was what we had waited for—our complete family, together at last.

I often observed my father, noticing how the Army had shaped him into the man he was. Loyalty, duty, respect, honour, integrity—these values were ingrained in him, evident in everything he did. He approached life with a problem-solving mind-set, always reminding us, "Every problem has a solution; you just have to find it."

What a father, I thought. What a love!

Meanwhile, my mother went about her morning, humming softly as she worked. Sometimes, my parents would sing together, their offbeat harmony filling the air with joy. I often teased, "How can a frog and a nightingale sing together?" They would laugh, shaking their heads at me.

Yes, we were finally complete.

I opened a window, and there was Rocky, staring at me with his hazy, love-filled eyes. My heart warmed at the sight of him.

Rocky had entered our lives just a day after my father's retirement. A tiny bundle of fur, barely a month and a half old, he had grown into a young and strong, loyal companion just in a year.

I blew him a flying kiss. He licked his mouth, wagging his tail as if he understood my love for him.

"Ever since my father retired, we thought of adding a rock star to our family. And here you are, Rocky," I whispered, my heart swelling. "You're more than a pet—you're a genuine member of our family."

My father adored him, taking him for walks every morning and evening. Rocky, in turn, followed him with unwavering devotion. Watching them together was a sight to behold.

"Myra," Mom called. "Breakfast is waiting for you."

"Yes, Mom," I said, turning away from the window, but not before giving Rocky another flying kiss. He whimpered, wagging his tail once more.

As we enjoyed our tea and breakfast, my father and Rocky left for their morning activities again. Rocky glanced back at me a couple of times, as if wanting me to join them. But he understood and moved on.

"Wagging his tail with that innocent look—it has a deep meaning," Mom mused and giggled. "He seems to be an adorable son."

I nodded, touched by her simple yet profound words.

For the past ten months or so, life had been bliss. We shared meals together, laughed, and lived every moment to its fullest. My father often said, "Every day is a brand-new day since I came home."

But happiness is never without its shadows. Even in the brightest moments, memories of past struggles linger. And one such moment, nearly a year ago had shaken me deeply. It was the day my entrance result was declared.

And yet, life had its trials.

As I sat there, sipping my tea, a memory from nearly a year ago surfaced, unbidden. The day my entrance results were declared still felt raw, a moment that had shaken me to my core.

I remembered the day my entrance result was declared almost a year ago, "My heart had sunk. My name was missing from the merit list—not because I had failed, but maybe because of political interference. Corruption had seeped into even the education system, crushing dreams of thousands under its weight. I clenched my fists, frustration welling up inside me. Was it really my performance, or was there something else at play."

I exhaled sharply, "Politics itself isn't dirty," I thought bitterly. "It's the people who make it so."

"My eyes scanned the result list once, twice, thrice. My name was missing. *My roll Number 1143—Missing.* I held my breath, scrolling back up, as if willing my name to appear. But no matter how many times I searched, it wasn't there."

I thought again, "For a long moment, I just stood there, heart pounding, mind blank. *What went wrong?* Had I miscalculated my performance?"

Disappointment settled in, but before the panic could consume me, I forced myself to breathe. This wasn't the end.

When I reached home, my mother was already waiting. One look at me, and she knew.

"You didn't get in," she said softly. It wasn't a question.

I shook my head.

She sat beside me, her hands warm over mine. "Myra, one rejection doesn't mean you won't be a teacher. There are other colleges, other opportunities. This dream isn't over."

She was right. *I just had to find another way.*

Days turned into weeks, and though my heart still ached from the rejection, I refused to sit idle. My dear parents encouraged me to apply elsewhere, and after careful research, I found another B.Ed. college accepting admissions—*Serene Wood B.Ed. College*, located in the southernmost part of Highland. It was a renowned institution in the bustling heart of the city, known for its excellence in teacher training. It wasn't my first choice, but dreams aren't built on first choices—they are built on perseverance.

Despite my disappointment, I never let my parents see my pain. I pressed on, determined to carve my own path. My father, ever perceptive, eventually understood the struggles I faced.

He often asked, "Are you happy, Myra?"

I would smile and say, "Dad, I'm more than happy. You and Mom are my world. You are the artery and the vein, and love is the blood that keeps us alive. What more could I ask for?"

He would smile back, a few wrinkles deepening on his face, but happiness lighting up his eyes.

A few days later, on a bright Sunday morning, my father returned from his walk with Rocky. The sky was clear, the world seemed at peace, more in the Highland and I realized something profound: No matter the hardships, love, family, and integrity would always triumph.

And that, above all, was the greatest gift of life.

And we all sat across the table—certainly not for tea this time. On my request, Dad, Mom, and the rock star followed me to the open porch, where the morning air felt a hundred times more refreshing. I wanted them to savour the beauty of the dawn, to breathe in its serenity.

They understood my unspoken desire, exchanged a knowing glance, and with a wink at each other, they made my heart swell with joy. Their love for my happiness made me feel like I was standing at the peak of the world.

Dad sat cross-legged on the chair, a familiar habit of his when deep in thought. Perhaps he was thinking about tea, I mused. The rock star, too, settled in comfortably. I knew Dad preferred coffee, sometimes even black tea, but that morning, I decided to prepare coffee for all of us. I wanted it to be special.

Adjusting his chair slightly, Dad took a long sip and sighed in contentment.

"It's great...!" he exclaimed, his voice carrying a warmth that wrapped around me like a soft embrace.

Mom nodded in agreement, her eyes twinkling. "She is just great," Dad added, shaking his head in admiration.

"She is," Mom affirmed, sharing a smile with him.

They both took another sip, their eyes meeting briefly before turning to me. When they smiled, a few wrinkles gently formed at the corners of Mom's eyes and near her lips—lines that spoke of years of love, laughter, and endurance. I glanced at Dad's face, searching for similar marks of time but found far fewer. Mom had Dad, and I had the rock star.

For me, they were as young as anyone, and I was lost in the warmth of our togetherness. Lately, I had noticed subtle changes in my father. He seemed to tire more easily, rubbing his temples as if battling a silent headache. But he never complained. "A soldier never shows weakness," he would say with a grin. I didn't think much of it at the time. Maybe I should have.

But suddenly, the moment shattered. Dad clutched his chest, his face contorting in pain. His breath hitched as he struggled, choking on his coffee.

"Dad!" I cried, my heart hammering against my ribs. Mom rushed to his side, her hands trembling as she tried to steady him.

Without wasting a second, we hurried him to the nearby Evergreen Serenity Hospital (ESH). The air felt thick with fear as we watched the doctors begin their work. Mom and I sat in the waiting room, our hands clenched together in silent prayer. We were not just worried about Dad's condition but also about the hospital's facilities.

"How can the doctors leave patients to their own fate?" I thought bitterly, my faith wavering.

After what felt like an eternity, a doctor finally emerged.

"Doctor," I blurted out, my voice raw with anxiety. "Is my father alright?"

The doctor nodded, but his expression was grave. "He's stable for now. But he needs to be transferred to a private hospital soon for better treatment."

A wave of relief and fear hit me at once.

"Thank you, Doctor. I just want my Dad to live."

"Don't worry," he reassured me before disappearing into another ward.

We rushed to Dad's side. He lay on the hospital bed, his eyes glistening with unshed tears. Seeing him like that—so vulnerable—broke something inside me. My throat tightened as I fought to keep my emotions at bay, but the dam burst. Mom, too, couldn't hold back her tears as she wiped his face gently. I could feel the pain he was going through.

The hospital was abuzz with murmurs about the lack of doctors and nurses, a topic that had become common not just in news reports but also in the whispers of the suffering. It was infuriating—people were losing their lives, not because their conditions were untreatable, but because of negligence on the part of authorities and a lack of medical facilities.

"Doctors aren't gods, but when they can save lives and fail to do so due to external constraints, it is a tragedy," I thought.

"I will be alright soon," Dad murmured, squeezing Mom's hand.

"We're not worried," Mom replied, though her tear-filled eyes betrayed her words. Dad kissed both our hands, his touch warm yet feeble.

That night, we prayed for his recovery. I informed Kesav and Nani over the phone, their voices were filled with worry. I assured them that all was well. Rocky, the rock star, sat quietly beside us, his eyes filled with understanding. He knew something was wrong. The news really shocked and hurt the family of Nani and Kesav and others in the Rani village.

The next day, Dad was transferred to City Private Hospital (CPH). Thanks to Kesav's help, everything was arranged swiftly. We hoped for the best, but fate had other plans. At first, Dad wanted to be shifted to the Army Hospital, but we managed at CPH.

The news hit us like a thunderbolt—Dad had survived, but he had lost hearing in his left ear with difficulty in speaking clearly. The doctor warned us that another heart attack could be fatal if he did not receive the best treatment available. No one had expected this outcome. Mom was shaken to her core, and I was left staring at the doctor in stunned silence.

Neighbours and well-wishers came to visit. Their presence was a source of comfort in our time of distress. We thanked them wholeheartedly for standing by us.

Two weeks later, Dad was discharged. We followed every instruction given by the doctors. Though he was home, he wasn't the same. Once strong and confident man now looked frail. Rocky, too, seemed to have sensed the change in his master.

We often discussed seeking further treatment in the Army Hospital, where retired officers received free and reliable medical care. A month later, we took him there. For the second time, the doctors gave us a ray of extreme hope. They assured us that with continued treatment, he could improve gradually.

And so, every three months, we took him to the Army Hospital. Slowly but surely, he responded well to the treatment. Life began returning to normal. Dad, a man who had spent 20 years in the Hindasia Army, understood struggle more than anyone else did. Despite everything, life carried on. My father, though changed, still faced each day with quiet strength. And in his eyes, I saw a lesson—not just about survival, but about perseverance.

Ties That Endure
Summary

Myra finds joy in her father's retirement, cherishing their newfound time together as a complete family. Their days are filled with warmth, laughter, and companionship, especially with Rocky, their loyal pet. However, memories of past struggles linger—particularly the heartbreak of being rejected and denied admission due to political interference. However, disappointment weighs heavily on her, her mother's unwavering support helps her push forward, leading her to an alternative path to achieve her dream of becoming a teacher.

Just as life settles into bliss, tragedy strikes when her father suffers a heart attack. The lack of proper medical facilities in the local hospital forces them to rush him to a private hospital, where he survives but is left with partial hearing loss and difficulty speaking. The once strong and disciplined Army man now appears fragile, yet his resilience remains.

With the unwavering support of family and well-wishers, they seek further treatment at the Army Hospital. Over time, he shows signs of improvement, proving that love, perseverance, and hope can triumph over even the darkest moments. Through these trials, Myra learns that struggles are inevitable, but the strength to overcome them lies in the bonds of family and the determination to keep moving forward.

20. Threads of Home and Hope

The morning sun streamed through the curtains of my room, casting a golden glow on the suitcase I had packed the night before. I sat cross-legged on the floor, surrounded by books, notebooks, and a few cherished mementos. The room felt smaller somehow, as if the walls had absorbed all the laughter, tears, and dreams of my childhood.

The next day, I would leave for my Serene Wood B.Ed. College, a step closer to my dream of becoming a teacher. But as I looked around, I couldn't help but feel the weight of the journey that had brought me here.

My fingers traced the edges of a faded photograph—my family, smiling under the shade of the old banyan tree in our garden. Rocky, our loyal dog, sat at our feet, his tail forever frozen mid-wag. I smiled, my heart swelling with gratitude. I had come so far, but I hadn't done it alone. Every step of the way, my family, my friends, and even the challenges had shaped me into the person I was then.

A Call from Nani

The sound of my phone buzzing broke my reverie. It was Nani. My face lit up as I answered the video call.

"Hey, Nani!" I greeted, my voice warm with affection.

"Myra! Are you all packed?" Nani's face filled the screen, her eyes sparkling with excitement. Behind her, the bustling streets of Dream City were a blur of activity.

"Almost," I replied, holding up a pair of shoes I was debating whether to pack. "I can't believe I'm actually leaving tomorrow."

"I'm so proud of you," Nani said, her voice softening. "You've worked so hard for this. Remember when we used to dream about the future back in school? Look at us now—you're becoming a teacher, and I'm a nurse. Who would've thought?"

I laughed, the sound tinged with nostalgia. "I still can't believe you're in Dream City. How's everything there?"

Nani sighed, leaning back in her chair. "It's busy, but I love it. The hospital keeps me on my toes, but it's rewarding. I've learned so much, and I feel like I'm finally making a difference. But I miss home. I miss you."

"I miss you too," I said, my voice catching. "But you're doing amazing things, Nani. You're living your dream."

"And so are you," Nani replied, her tone firm. "Don't ever forget that. You've always been the strongest person I know."

Before I could respond, Madhu Aunt's face appeared on the screen, her smile as warm as ever. "Myra, Naani! How are you?"

"I'm good, Auntie," I said, my heart swelling at the sight of her. "Just packing for yet another college, another city."

"Ah, college," Madhu Aunt said, her eyes twinkling. "I remember when you and Nani were little girls, running around the village, dreaming big dreams. And now look at you—both of you are making those dreams come true."

I felt a lump form in my throat. "It's because of you and Mom that we've come this far. You've always believed in us."

Madhu Aunt waved her hand dismissively, but I could see the pride in her eyes. "We just gave you the tools, Naani. You're the ones who built your futures. And don't worry—Highland will always be here, waiting for you to come back and make it even better."

Later that evening, as the sun dipped below the horizon. I sat on the porch, a letter in my hands. It was from Kesav. I unfolded it carefully, my heart racing as I began to read:

"My dearest Myra,

As I sit here writing to you, I can't help but think about tomorrow—the day you leave for your B.Ed. course. I wish I could be there to see you off, to stand by your side as you take this brave step toward your dreams. But even though I can't be there in person, please know that I'm with you in spirit, cheering you on every step of the way.

Myra, you've always been an inspiration to me. Your strength, your determination, and your unwavering belief in doing what's right—these are the qualities that make you so extraordinary. You've faced so many challenges, yet you've never let anything dim your light. And now, as you embark on this new journey, I know you'll shine even brighter.

I've been doing a lot of thinking lately, about my own dreams and the path I want to take. You know how much I've always admired your father—his courage, his dedication, and the way he served our nation with pride. His stories of Army life have stayed with me, and over time, I've realized that I want to follow in his footsteps. The Army isn't just a career for me; it's a calling. It's about serving something greater than myself, about protecting the people and the country I love.

I know this path won't be easy. It will demand sacrifices, and there will be times when I'll be far away from the people I care about most—like you. But I also know that it's a journey worth taking. And just as your father's service inspired *me, I hope that one day, my journey will inspire others too.*

Myra, as you step into this new chapter of your life, I want you to know how proud I am of you. You've always been my source of strength, and I have no doubt that you'll achieve incredible things. And when the time comes for me to join the Army, I'll carry your love and support with me, just as I hope you'll carry mine with you now.

No matter where life takes us, remember this: you're never alone. I'm here, always, rooting for you.

With all my love,
Kesav"

I folded the letter, my eyes glistening with tears. I held it close to my heart, feeling the warmth of his words. Kesav had always been my anchor, my source of strength. And even though he couldn't be there in person, his love was a constant presence in my life.

A Family Farewell

The next morning, the house was filled with a mix of excitement and bittersweet emotions. My parents helped me load my suitcase into the car, while Rocky trotted beside us, his tail wagging furiously.

"Are you sure you have everything?" my mother asked, her voice tinged with worry.

"Yes, Mom," I replied, smiling. "I've checked a hundred times."

My father placed a hand on my shoulder, his eyes filled with pride. "You're going to do great, Myra. Just remember—no matter where you go, you carry Highland with you. And you carry our love."

I nodded, my throat tight with emotion. "I'll make you proud, Dad. I promise." I said.

As we got ready, the conversation turned to the future. I shared my hopes for my B.Ed. program, my dreams of becoming a teacher who could inspire change. My parents listened intently, their faces glowing with pride.

"And you have a way of seeing the best in everyone," Dad added. "That's what makes you special, Myra. You don't just teach—you inspire."

Now, I knelt down to say goodbye to Rocky. He nuzzled my hand, his eyes filled with an understanding that only a loyal companion could have.

"Take care of them for me, okay?" I whispered, scratching behind his ears. "I'll be back soon."

My father placed a hand on my shoulder, his touch firm but gentle. "Myra," he said, his voice a little softer than before, "remember what I've always told you—life is about moving forward, no matter how hard it gets. You've seen me struggle, but I'm still here, still fighting. And so will you."

I looked into his eyes, seeing the determination that had carried him through his recovery.

"You've taught me so much, Dad," I said, my voice breaking. "Not just with your words, but with your strength. I'll carry that with me, always." He pulled me into a hug, his arms strong and steady. "You will make us proud, Myra," he whispered. "And remember, we're just a phone call away."

I turned to my mother, who had been quietly watching us, her eyes glistening with unshed tears. She stepped forward and cupped my face in her hands. "Myra, my dear," she said, her voice trembling but filled with love, "you've always been our shining star. Don't ever forget how much we believe in you."

I hugged her tightly, breathing in the familiar scent of her perfume, a mix of jasmine and home. "I'll miss you, Mom," I whispered. "Take care of Dad and Rocky for me."

She nodded, pulling back to look at me with a smile.

Rocky barked softly, as if to say, "I will," and I couldn't help but smile through my tears.

The driver, who had been patiently waiting by the car, cleared his throat gently. "It's time, Myra," he said, his tone kind but firm.

I took a deep breath, standing up and wiping my tears. My parents stood side by side, their arms around each other, their faces a mix of pride and sadness. Rocky sat at their feet, his eyes fixed on me.

"I love you all," I said, my voice steady despite the lump in my throat. "I'll call as soon as I reach."

My father nodded, his eyes shining with pride. "We love you too, Myra. Go and show the world what you're made of."

With one last wave, I turned and followed the driver to the car. As we drove away, I looked back through the window, watching my parents and Rocky grow smaller in the distance. My heart ached, but it was also full—full of love, of gratitude, and of the strength, they had given me.

My Realization

At the bus station, I leaned back in my seat, my heart full. I thought about Nani, Madhu Aunt, Kesav and his ever letter, my parents, and star– Rocky. They were all threads in the tapestry of my life, each one contributing to the person I had become.

I realized that my journey wasn't just about me—it was about the collective strength of my family, my friends, and my community. It was about the lessons I had learned, the challenges I had overcome, and the love that had carried me through.

As the bus rolled through the familiar streets of Highland, I felt a renewed sense of purpose. I was ready to face the challenges ahead, to learn, to grow, and to one day return to Highland as a teacher who could inspire the next generation.

I closed my eyes, a small smile playing on my lips. The journey ahead would be challenging, but I was ready. For the first time, I felt truly at peace, knowing that no matter where life took me, I would always carry the echoes of Highland with me.

Threads of Home and Hope Summary

Myra prepares to leave for her B.Ed. college, surrounded by the warmth of her family and the comforting presence of Rocky, their loyal dog. As she packs, she reflects on the journey that has brought her here, feeling gratitude for the support of her parents, Nani, Madhu Aunt, and Kesav, whose heartfelt letter inspires her with his dreams of joining the Army. The next morning, her parents bid her an emotional farewell, reminding her to carry Highland's love and lessons with her wherever she goes.

As Myra departs, she realizes her journey isn't just about her—it's shaped by the collective strength of her family, friends, and community. With a renewed sense of purpose, she sets off, ready to face the challenges ahead and one day return as a teacher who inspires the next generation. The echoes of Highland, filled with love and resilience, remain a constant presence in her heart.

21. The Weight of Knowledge

Six months had flown by since I left for my B.Ed. College, and now I was home in Highland for a brief visit. The scent of my mother's cooking filled the air, and the sound of Rocky's excited barks echoed through the house. It felt good to be back, even if only for a few weeks, surrounded by the familiar warmth of my family and the comforting rhythms of home. Yet, even in this peaceful setting, my mind often wandered to the lessons I had learned and the questions that still lingered—especially with my couple of semesters looming ahead.

One autumn evening, as I sat curled up on the porch with a cup of tea, I reached for a literature book I hadn't touched in months. The crisp air carried the faint scent of fallen leaves, and the golden light of the setting sun bathed everything in a soft glow. Flipping through the pages, I stumbled upon a quote that stopped me in my tracks: *"To know is to know that you know nothing. That is the meaning of true knowledge."* —Socrates.

I read it aloud, the words hanging in the air like a challenge. They struck a chord deep within me, shifting my perspective in a way I hadn't expected. Learning, I realized, wasn't just about collecting facts or mastering subjects. It was about humility, about recognizing the vastness of what I didn't know and embracing the journey of discovery.

I read it twice and thrice before I truly grasped its depth. Excited, I ran to Mom and Dad, eager to discuss it with them. They laughed at first, then became so engrossed in our conversation that they declared themselves followers of all those great minds and litterateurs especially of Socrates from that day forward.

Seeing an Army man reading philosophy was a new sight for me, but it was also inspiring. That evening, I decided to write. I picked up my pen and diary, but nothing came to mind. My thoughts were blank—wiped clean by the profundity of Socrates' words.

After a few moments of contemplation, I scribbled down my thoughts:

1. "I prefer humanity to all kinds of inspirations."
2. "Every teacher is good at one thing. As a good student, find that one thing and learn from it."
3. "Democracy is the inspiration for living."
4. "The word 'humanity' is immense in any learning."
5. "One should always strive to find their place in the world of understanding."
6. "Politeness is the acceptance of learning."
7. "Humanity is yet another inspiration of my life."
8. "Understanding 'humanity' can save the world from its fragility."
9. "To learn is to learn how to learn."
10. "Acceptance is the beginning of learning."

I read my words again and smiled.

"Maybe they are okay. I made it," I thought.

Writing had given me clarity. I realized how hard it was to come up with something meaningful. Every quote held a deep truth.

As exhaustion took over, I lay down, hugging my pillow tight.

"I have fallen in love with a literary romance after so long," I thought again, blushing. The words on the page had stirred something deep within me, something I hadn't felt in years.

Before sleep claimed me, one thought lingered in my mind—

How could I become a good teacher? When am I completing the course?

The question echoed in my dreams, where a classroom full of eager yet misguided students awaited my guidance.

And in that dream, I knew—

Teaching wasn't just about imparting knowledge. It was about igniting a fire in young minds, guiding them to think beyond the ordinary, and, above all, helping them find meaning in the vast expanse of life.

A few students were brilliant and not useless, as some of them spoke good English and carried themselves with self-confidence. They were aware of the latest news, innovations, and technological advancements. Yet, the irony was that even they had set their hearts on fat pay packages without possessing the skills necessary to earn that much.

There was no culture of extra reading, and many students were completely lost in class. Quality education seemed absent in the school, and I suspected that this was the case in many other institutions as well.

When I asked them questions about subjects they had studied in the last few years, they struggled to recall anything. As for novels, articles, and magazines, those were completely out of the question. When asked about ethics, culture, literature, and behaviour, they fumbled and hesitated. The very mention of the word 'literature' seemed to terrify them the most.

Some students displayed unethical behaviour, their actions lacking any sense of decorum. They craved readymade answers, unwilling to engage in critical thinking. They would enthusiastically declare their commitment to hard work and success, yet their words lacked conviction. I found myself frustrated by their rehearsed and shallow responses.

I wondered, "Has time produced a generation whose sole objective is to live comfortably, earn a fortune, but without contributing anything meaningful?" When I pushed them further, they simply repeated the same empty phrases. Those who spoke of genuine ideas were laughed at, mocked for being 'old-fashioned.'

The classroom began to blur, the students' voices fading into a distant hum. I felt a gentle tug, as if the dream itself was unraveling. The faint scent of jasmine wafted through the air, pulling me back to reality.

"Myra," I heard my mother's voice, soft but insistent. "It's dinner time. Please wake up."

I blinked, the classroom dissolving into the familiar walls of my room. The remnants of the dream lingered like a whisper, the students' faces still vivid in my mind.

"Okay, Mom," I murmured, my eyes still closed. I realized that it had all been a dream.

"Even my dreams are haunting me now," I thought.

A lesson I needed to learn.
"What an uneasy dream!" I sighed, rubbing my forehead and adjusting my hair.

"What an uneasy dream!" I thought again.

"Teaching is not an easy aspiration, Mom," I said aloud. "I saw something troubling in my dream."

"Oh?" she said. "Don't worry too much. Everything will be fine. Your father is doing better too. Our prayers will be answered."

"Was it just a dream?" I asked myself, still unsettled. "How can that be so real?"

"Yes, Myra," Mom reassured me. "Take it easy. Dreams reflect our worries sometimes."

"Maybe you're right, Mom," I said, finally sitting up. "Let's have dinner."

As we sat around the dining table, my father, looking much better, greeted me with a smile.

"Where were you, Myra?" he asked eagerly. "Thank you for all your love for me".

"She was dreaming," Mom answered, not forgetting to smile as always. I did not particularly like that response, but I let it slide.

"Dreaming? Is it a daydream?" Dad repeated, raising an eyebrow.

"Yes, Dad..." I started to explain, "Sometimes, our dreams reflect reality." I somehow imitated Mom's thought. Although, it was a *siesta dream,* but it reflected reality of Highland in many different ways.

"Is something bothering you, my dear?" he asked, his voice filled with concern.

"No, Dad," I replied a bit louder so he could hear me clearly. My mother gave me a knowing glance, aware that my father's hearing had been affected, making it slightly difficult for him to respond to voices around him. But he simply smiled and continued serving the food. I had never seen my parents argue in my entire life. Their life together was an example of harmony, love, and understanding—qualities that many in our society could learn from.

"But I liked that quote," Dad said suddenly, laughing. "In fact, we both loved it."

"Yes, it was wonderful," Mom agreed, assisting him. I joined in as well. Soon, we were all gathered around the table, and even Rocky, our loyal rock star, sat patiently by our side, knowing it was a moment of togetherness.

That night, as I lay in bed, I read '*Ulysses*' by Alfred Lord Tennyson. The poem filled me with countless emotions—thoughts of my journey, my family, my education, my inspirations, and even the political state of Hindasia. It also made me reflect on loss and mortality.

"What a poem!" I whispered to myself. "Good night."

"Tomorrow, I will try to be a better learner—so that one day, I can be a better teacher," I thought, pulling the pillows closer.

The Weight of Knowledge Summary

Myra, home for a brief visit after six months at her B.Ed. college, finds herself reflecting on the true meaning of learning. While flipping through a literature book, she stumbles upon a quote by Socrates: "To know is to know that you know nothing." The quote deeply resonates with her, shifting her perspective on knowledge and teaching. Inspired, she writes down her thoughts, exploring themes like humanity, learning, and the role of a teacher.

That night, Myra has a vivid dream about a classroom filled with students who lack curiosity, critical thinking, and a genuine desire to learn. The dream troubles her, as she witnesses the challenges of modern education—students focused on material success rather than meaningful growth. Waking up, she shares her concerns with her parents, who reassure her and remind her of the importance of perseverance.

The chapter ends with Myra reading Tennyson's *Ulysses*, which fills her with a renewed sense of purpose. She resolves to continue her journey of learning, determined to one day become a teacher who inspires and ignites a love for knowledge in her students.

22. A Dream Amidst Chaos

A few weeks later, I woke up with the weight of yet another dream still pressing on my mind. Was it merely a dream, or was it trying to tell me something? Shaking off the thoughts, I stepped out into the crisp morning air, hoping to find clarity in the routine of the day.

I followed my usual routine—watering the flowers in the garden, cleaning the surroundings, and helping my mother in the kitchen. The flowers seemed to smile in the gentle morning light, and their fragrance lifted my spirits. As I inhaled deeply, I thought, "Flowers bloom with joy, just as a family thrives in love. Parents are like a garden, nurturing their children."

But amidst the tranquility, my mind wandered to the upcoming semester. In just a few days, I would be heading back to college, leaving behind the comfort of home once again. The thought filled me with a mix of excitement and apprehension—excitement for the new lessons and experiences awaiting me, and apprehension about the challenges I would face. Still, I reminded myself that this was all part of the journey, a step closer to my dream of becoming a teacher who could inspire change.

I saw my father going for his morning walk, with Rocky wagging his tail happily behind him. He waved at me, and for a moment, it felt like all was right in the world.

Certainly, he had improved now.

As I wiped my hands after finishing in the kitchen, I heard the sharp voice of a news anchor from the television, "Mass protests continue across Highland as citizens demand reforms in education and governance."

Curious, I stepped closer, but before I could listen further, loud chants from outside caught my attention. I walked to the gate and saw crowds gathering, their voices rising in unison.

That afternoon, we witnessed a massive protest rally not only on the streets of Highland against its authority but also against the ruling governments of various other states in the country. The Protest was also broadcast on Televisions and Radios capturing the nationwide attention.

The entire state was in turmoil, with people demanding reforms in education, governance, and the fight against random corruption all over. General election was approaching, and political debates dominated television, print as well as social media. While some media houses remained unbiased, others blatantly supported their desired parties, spinning narratives to protect them rather than hold it accountable.

I saw the stark contrast in society—the poor becoming poorer while the rich amassed even greater wealth. Promises were all over in the ears of Highland. However, their actions betrayed them literally. Books were published with titles like 'Social Justice,' 'Good Governance,' and 'Champion of Democracy,' 'Best education system in Highland', yet the people continued to suffer at the grassroots level. They could have governed democratically with fairness, transparency, and a commitment to the well-being of all citizens.

Every night, my mind swirled with thoughts—education, democracy, governance, and society. I was a young woman. Perhaps I should have been thinking about love, romance, or finding a life partner. But the disheartening situation in the state weighed heavily on me.

I often discussed these issues with my parents and friends, but most people chose silence over confrontation. Fear gripped them and some believed democracy was a myth, an illusion for the poor. Others said, women should remain confined to their homes and not engage in politics. "It's not a woman's place," they insisted.

Some even whispered, "Better to stay quiet than to risk losing our livelihood. Politics is dangerous." But I couldn't stay quiet. Not when so much was at stake.

My dream, both literal and metaphorical, was clear—to become a teacher who could inspire change, who could instil critical thinking in students, who could nurture minds to question and analyse rather than accept blindly. But was it possible in a society where education was neglected, where political freedom was stifled, where people feared speaking their truth?

I did not have all the answers. But I knew one thing—I couldn't stop dreaming. Because dreams, after all, are where revolutions begin.

The grievances were reported everywhere and people expressed that they were discriminated against based on caste, religion, beliefs, social status, and, most importantly, their choice of political parties. Sometimes, I wished the ruling government could understand that governance is meant for all—not just for those who voted them into power, but also for those who did not.

Moreover, I had never realized until then that democracy was not always as strong as I had believed. It could be influenced by wealth, swayed by power, and even reshaped by those who controlled the system. The poor were often obliged to sell their rights due to genuine struggles such as poverty and a lack of awareness about their fundamental human and political rights.

I often pondered, "Democracy grants us the right to enjoy, cherish, and hope for a better life. It adds meaning to existence and ensures our basic human rights. But where are those rights? Where are those values of humanity?"

Of course, there were no answers. Perhaps those who dared to ask were not in a position to receive answers. Or maybe, had I held a position in the ruling government, I would have understood better. Elections were approaching, and various regional and national parties campaigned fervently. They all claimed to seek change—a better future for the next generation. Yet, almost every day, I heard conflicting slogans like "Jindabad (Long live democracy!)" or "Murdabad (Down with corruption!)" on the streets of Evergreen and sometimes even in Rani Village, outside my home. These same slogans echoed on TV, and other social media platforms. I realized how deeply politics had infiltrated everyday life.

My parents often warned me against engaging in politics. They advised me not to join rallies or campaigns, for they had seen the struggles people endured and the consequences of becoming victims of their own rights. Nothing felt right or fulfilling. My future seemed uncertain amid the turbulent political landscape of the Highland. "Nature has blessed us with everything—pure water, fresh air, and breath-taking beauty. But why must the political environment be so different?" I often wondered.

No one encouraged me to be part of politics. Yet, for me, it seemed the only path to achieving my lifelong dream of becoming a teacher. Perhaps, if I remained true to my purpose rather than pursuing personal political gain, I could make a difference. The overwhelming thoughts and mental turmoil left me restless, but my determination remained unwavering.

Change had to begin somewhere. And maybe, just maybe, a classroom was as good a place as any other. Its echoes had to reach in the Highland, carrying the promise of the better tomorrow.

A Dream Amidst Chaos Summary

Myra wakes up haunted by a lingering dream, unsure whether it holds a deeper meaning. Seeking solace in her morning routine, she reflects on the love and care of her parents, comparing them to a garden that nurtures its flowers.

As she prepares to leave for college, she feels both excitement and apprehension. While she looks forward to new lessons and experiences, she also worries about the challenges ahead. However, she reassures herself that each step brings her closer to her dream of becoming a teacher who can inspire change. Protests erupt across the streets, demanding reforms in education, governance, and corruption.

As election season approaches, political debates dominate the media, and Myra becomes increasingly aware of the stark inequalities in society. She struggles with the realization that democracy often favors the powerful while leaving the poor unheard.

Despite warnings from her parents and society to stay away from politics—especially as a woman—Myra finds herself unable to ignore the injustice around her. She questions whether silence is truly the answer when so much is at stake. While others believe politics is dangerous, she sees it as deeply connected to education and change. Her dream of becoming a teacher is no longer just about academics; it is about shaping young minds to think critically and challenge the system.

23. A Dream Fulfilled

Time moved forward, carrying me along its steady current. Dreams that once felt distant were now within reach, though the path had not been as simple as I had imagined. Ever since my days at APS, I had carried the dream of becoming a teacher—of standing in a classroom just like Miss Nidhi, shaping young minds the way she had shaped mine. After completing my degree in English Literature and a Bachelor of Education from *Serene Wood B.Ed. College*, I knew it was time to turn that dream into reality.

Finding a teaching job, however, wasn't as easy as I had imagined. I spent weeks searching, filling out applications, and hoping for an opportunity. Then, one day, I came across a vacancy in a school at *Government Starlight Mission School*, beyond the eastern hills of Highland, in a small town where teachers were scarce, yet students were eager to learn. Without a second thought, I applied.

When I received the interview call, a wave of emotions swept over me—excitement, nervousness, anticipation. On the day of the interview, as I sat before the panel, I spoke with all my heart open. I shared how my love for teaching had begun, how I believed education could change lives, and how I hoped to make a difference. Every word I said was filled with sincerity, and when I was offered the position, I knew I had taken my first step toward fulfilling my purpose.

The first day at school was overwhelming yet beautiful. As I walked into the classroom, dozens of curious eyes followed me. The room was small, the resources limited, but I saw something far greater—potential. Taking a deep breath, I smiled and introduced myself. I started the lesson with a story, just as Miss Nidhi used to, drawing them in with every word. Slowly, I saw their expressions change, their confidence build over the years.

At that moment, felt a deep sense of fulfilment and I realized—I was no longer just Myra, the girl with a dream. I was Myra, the teacher, carrying forward the legacy of knowledge, wisdom, hope and change.

As the school bus slowed down to a stop near my house, I gathered my bag and stepped down, feeling the familiar warmth of home settle in my heart. The evening sun cast a golden glow over the Highland, and a cool breeze carried the distant aroma of blooming rhododendrons.

Before I could take a couple of more steps, a tiny figure broke into a run. "Mummy!" Little Nidhi's voice rang through the air, her small arms outstretched. I knelt just in time to catch her, her soft curls brushing against my cheek as she giggled.

Behind her, Mom and Dad stood at the gate, their faces beaming with joy. Even Rocky, our ever-loyal dog, wagged his tail in excitement, circling around us as always.

"You're home, finally! How was your day at school?" asked Mom.

I smiled, pressing a kiss to my angel's forehead. "It was wonderful, as always– a day I had dreamed of, for so many years."

As I spoke, my mind drifted back to the challenges I faced throughout my degrees especially Bachelor of Education. The journey from earning my degree to finally standing in a classroom was never easy. It was filled with uncertainty, countless transitions, and struggles that tested my resilience at every step. There were endless applications, rejections, and moments when doubt crept in, making the dream feel impossibly distant sometimes. Yet, I kept pushing forward, refusing to let setbacks define me. And now, as I stood here with my little girl in my arms, I knew that every hardship, every challenge had shaped me into the teacher I had always dreamed of becoming.

Dad chuckled and smiled in pride. "And did your students drive you crazy today?"

I laughed, shaking my head. "Not as much as this little one does." I tickled little Nidhi, making her burst into fits of laughter. As we walked home together, I felt a deep sense of contentment. This—this simple, beautiful moment—was everything I had ever dreamed of.

My little angel, Nidhi, was the best friend of her grandparents.

Walking down home, Mom said, "She doesn't need you anymore."

She smiled, waiting for my reaction. I knew how much Mom had cared for Nidhi since the day she was born. I nodded in agreement, feeling immense gratitude.

"Miss Nidhi once showed me the power of knowledge, and now, as I have my own little Nidhi in my life, I see the future I once dreamed of. She carries a name that shaped my past, and perhaps one day, she too will change the world in her own way," I thought filled with pride and contentment.

I looked at Nidhi. She gave me an innocent smile and curled her fingers, as if calling me, just like nature calls from the Highland's Himalayas. Her innocence and beauty made me realize what it meant to be a mother.

"Life had come full circle.," I realized again. I was no longer just a student, nor just a teacher—I was a mother, a daughter, and a believer in a brighter tomorrow.

And in my arms, I held the future.

"She is the greatest gift of my life," I thought. "Life has taught me so much, and today, it has transformed me in countless ways."

Inside, we sat across the table, playing with Nidhi and Rocky. The real rock star, Rocky, had grown strong and protective, serving as Nidhi's personal guardian. He cared for her deeply, licking her face in affection, making her giggle with joy sometimes.

"Ever since she was born, my mother has been her true mother," I reflected. We spent one of the best evenings ever, having a special evening tea and snacks.

"So, ma'am," Dad asked, breaking the conversation, "how is your teaching life?" His voice carried the same warmth, but I couldn't help noticing the subtle signs of time etched onto his face. A few more wrinkles had deepened around his eys, his hair had thinned and turned a shade greyer, and faint crisscross lines marked his forehead—silent testaments to the years that had passed. Yet, his eyes still held the same pride and curiosity that had always reassured me.

"Everything is fine, Dad. Every day is a new day, a new opportunity to shape the young minds and inspire change, filled with learning experiences. Teaching isn't just a profession for me –it's a way of empowering the students to think, question and dream."

"I am forever grateful for the support you gave me all these past years. You fought the election, you won, and you stood by my aspirations. Now, we have a new government, new administration, and decision-makers who truly care. The people of Highland are content, and for the first time, there are no dissatisfied voices against the current ruling government," I added with a sense of relief and gratitude.

I continued holding my little Nidhi, "The education system has significantly improved over the last few years. Government schools are now competing with private institutions in providing quality education. And look at the infrastructures! They are simply remarkable–modern, well equipped, truly impressive! Despite these transformations, I know my purpose remains here. I can make a difference."

Dad listened intently, while I passed Nidhi onto his lap. She smiled, showing her two tiny teeth, and we all laughed in delight.

"We are happy that you are happy with what you do," Mom said warmly.

"Yes, we are," Dad added proudly. "And that was our dream too."

My father had the presence of an army man more than that of a politician. His disciplined life and unwavering integrity inspired me—not just as a daughter, but also as a teacher and a mother.

Nidhi stretched her little hands toward me, and I laughed, embracing her joy. Watching my parents' happiness over Nidhi and her innocence was a moment I cherished deeply. Throughout their lives, my parents never argued. They always stood as pillars of love and unity, and I was their witness.

Mom often said, "You have brought even more happiness into our family, Myra, with the birth of Nidhi."

Lost in reminiscence, I thought, "Three years have passed since Kesab and I tied the knot—a simple yet beautiful ceremony in the presence of our loved ones. Life took me on a path I had never imagined. Not only was I a teacher, but I was also the wife of an Army officer. The transition had been both challenging and rewarding. Our wedding wasn't just a union of two souls, but a promise to stand by each other, no matter where life took us. The farewell from my home had been filled with bittersweet emotions—tears from my parents, joy from my friends, and a deep sense of belonging to the man I had chosen. When I first arrived at the Army quarters, the structured yet warm world of the military welcomed me. And amid it all, my dream of teaching in Highland remained steadfast."

That night, as the cool Highland breeze drifted through my window, I reached for my phone. It had been a couple of days since I last heard Kesab's voice. Three years in the Army had taken him across different terrains, yet he remained the steady force in my life.

The call connected, and the moment I heard his voice, warmth spread through me.

"Myra," he said, his tone both gentle and firm.

"Kesab, I miss you," I whispered, feeling the weight of the distance between us.

A soft chuckle came from the other end. "I miss you too. How's my little troublemaker?"

"Sleeping soundly," I said, glancing at Nidhi. "She's growing up so fast, Kesab. Sometimes, I wish time would slow down."

"I know," he sighed. "I hate missing out on these moments. But duty calls, Myra. You understand that better than anyone."

I nodded, even though he couldn't see me. "I do. But that doesn't mean it's easy."

There was a pause before he spoke again. "I have news, love."

My heart skipped a beat. "What is it?"

"I'm coming home," he said, his voice filled with quiet excitement. "Just a few more weeks."

"For how long?"

"Long enough to make up for lost time," he assured me. "To be with you, with Nidhi. To watch her fall asleep in my arms instead of just hearing about it from you."

Tears welled up in my eyes. "That's the best news I've heard in a long time."

"I'll be counting down the days," he murmured.

"So will I," I whispered, holding the phone close as if it could shorten the miles between us.

At that moment, the distance didn't seem so unbearable. Hope had a way of bridging even the farthest gaps, and love—our love—was always strong enough to endure.

A Dream Fulfilled Summary

Myra reflects on her journey from being a young girl inspired by Miss Nidhi to becoming a teacher herself. The path wasn't easy—filled with struggles, transitions, and self - doubt—but her determination led her to *Government Starlight Mission School* in Highland, where she found her purpose.

As she returns home from work, she's welcomed by her parents and little Nidhi, a moment of warmth and fulfilment. Over an evening conversation, she shares her gratitude for her father's support and her commitment to shaping young minds.

Later that night, lost in reminiscence, Myra thinks about the last three years—her marriage to Kesab, the challenges of being a teacher, wife, and a mother. Feeling the distance, she calls Kesab, who has been away on duty. Their conversation is filled with longing, love, and hope, ending with the happiest news—Kesab is coming home soon.

24. The State's Transformation

Change doesn't arrive with a grand announcement—it creeps in, settling into the cracks of everyday life, waiting for the right moment to shatter everything you thought was certain.

It had been six months since my love last visited home. He had joined the Hindasia Army just before our marriage, shortly after I completed my degree from Serene Wood B.Ed. College, at a time when the election campaign in the Highland was at its peak.

Whenever he returned, once or twice in a year I would tease him, "How does Army life compare to being a taxi driver?" He would put on his old goggles, laugh, and say nothing but only smile.

I called him almost quite frequently if not every day, sharing stories about our family and Nidhi, our little angel. Whenever I worried about him, Dad reassured me, saying, "Army life is tough, but he is a good man. Be proud of him."

Little Nidhi's proud father would joke, "I wish I was still driving at Evergreen Marg. At least I could see you more often."

Sometimes, our conversations grew emotional, reminiscing about our past.

One day, I asked him, "Am I the right person for you?"

He smiled and replied, "I have the same question for you."

We understood how deeply we loved and respected each other. Any relationship, I believed, needed both love and respect to survive. Our journey had been shaped by the situations life presented to us, and I knew we had responded to those challenges well. Perhaps we were destined to be together forever.

Kesav had probably thought of another special name for his little angel, but I had named her. "Each time I call her name, I relive the memories of APS," I often thought. My mother would say that Nidhi's eyes were quite similar to those of her father, while her nose and lips resembled mine.

My eyes fell upon the newspapers on the table, both in regional language and English. I picked up the *Nature Express* and read the headline:

"Suicide Rate in Highland Drastically Declines Under the New Government: Agency's Survey Claims."

Flipping the page, another headline caught my attention:

"The Current Education System Has Transformed Lives in Highland."

Excitedly, I read aloud:

"Highland has become one of the country's exemplary states, receiving praise nationally and globally. Under the leadership of new Chief Minister Mr. N.B.S., the state has achieved remarkable progress across various sectors."

"Highland has earned numerous awards for quality education from primary to university levels, improved public transport, enhanced healthcare, grassroots

development, effective administration, employment generation, and a significant reduction in the suicide rate almost down to zero. Various national and international agencies have recognized these accomplishments of the state, Highland," I read again.

As I finished reading, emotions overwhelmed me. I smiled repeatedly and looked at my parents, seeking their validation.

"Yes, they are right," My Dad said.

"Yes, Dad," I agreed. "Those challenging days seem to have gone forever now."

"And better days are approaching," he added. "People have witnessed the best governance in Highland's history." I knew this to be true. My mother nodded with a warm smile.

"Dad, my dream has come true," I said. "I'm proud to be a citizen of Highland, and even more, a proud citizen of the world."

"You should be," Mom said. "This sort of governance is the one I always dreamed of."

"Indeed," Dad added. "I'm proud of this government in so many ways. Thanks to the establishment of an excellent, a world - class hospital, I regained my hearing completely. Now, I can receive treatment in my own state as and when I like. I can live—and die—with dignity."

"He is a leader of vision," Mom said. "Our CM Sahab, has eventually transformed Highland and the lives of its people. Look back five or ten years, and you will see the world of difference."

Dad looked at me as if ensuring I wasn't confused. Yes, I wasn't.

"Yes, I know," I replied.

"She is the mother of Nidhi," Mom reminded him.

"Oh yes, I forgot," Dad said, chuckling, and then laughing.

"Today, every village has 24/7 electricity and clean drinking water. All the educational institutions have their innovative libraries and even some of the modern villages got '*The Enlightenment Corner*', and they eradicated poverty down to almost zero. Of course, the hospitals have fully equipped medical facilities, with doctors available round the clock."

"And look at the roads," Mom added, her voice filled with awe. "They are world-class. Businesses thrive, tourism flourishes, and national media houses are setting up in our state. Literature and culture are now celebrated in every community."

"That's true," I agreed, glancing outside as a sleek tourist bus passed by. "Media plays a vital role in the state's all-round development. It helps share our stories, our struggles, and our victories with the rest of the country."

I thought back to the Highland I had grown up in—a place where poor infrastructure, lack of resources, and political negligence had held us back. But now, everything felt different. The streets were alive with possibilities.

Restaurants and Home Stays bustled with visitors, bookshops displayed exceptional works by some local authors, and the laughter of children echoed from well-maintained parks.

Dad, who had remained quiet, finally spoke. "It's not just about infrastructure, Myra. It's about hope and journey of complete transformation. The voice of the younger generation is being heard and appreciated everywhere in Highland. They believe in change because they have seen it happen."

I nodded, absorbing his words and thought, "It's all true. This is not just development—it is a transformation of mind-sets. We are no longer just people surviving in the Highland; we are now – the dreamers, achievers, and storytellers shaping the future of Hindasia."

My angel, little Nidhi loved on the laps of her grandparents. Her tiny fingers were trying to reach out for me. I held her close now, breathing in her familiar warmth, while listening to my parents' interesting conversation. Even Rocky, our ever-loyal companion, wagged his tail excitedly, as if he, too, wanted to join in. For us, he wasn't just a pet but a cherished member of the family, sharing in our joys and comforting us in our sorrows.

"Government is for all," my father said. "It serves those who voted for it and those who did not. No one should be deprived because of their human rights, more than the political ones."

"A government holds power to make decisions," he continued, "but it must ensure no discrimination."

I wondered at my father's evolving political awareness. Over the years, politics had influenced every individual's life.

"Yes," Mom added. "A government is for everyone. Politicians are in power because people elected them."

Curious, I wanted to hear more. They spoke as if they were politicians, and I was their audience in an assembly. My father was one of them and his life influenced ours. Somehow, we considered Rocky, as the political member of our family. We were informed citizens of the state, no doubt. I was one of the proudest daughters of a cabinet Minister in Highland!

"Can I say something?" I asked seriously.

They exchanged glances and chuckled, knowing I hadn't listened to their points. Nidhi listened quietly, playing with all herself, though it was too early for her to join in.

"Yes," Dad said. "Go ahead."

"Yes, Myra," Mom encouraged.

I began,

"I'm grateful to live in this country and of course, in this state of Highland. I remember the struggles we faced in the past due to political instability. The government's decisions impacted every aspect of our lives. At times, we nearly lost our hopes of our dreamed land. Young minds were misled and used by political parties for their own agendas. Many had no choice but to join their rallies."

I continued, "But now, everything has changed. The system has transformed. People's lives have improved significantly, and the education system has reached new heights. It has been three years since I entered my dream profession, and I can see the greatest transformation in Highland's history."

"Everything is great now," Dad said, smiling. "Am I right, ma'am?"

We all laughed. Nidhi, my little angel, joined in, along with our handsome, Rocky.

And dear readers, at that moment, I missed him.

The State's Transformation Summary

Six months had passed since Kesav's last visit home, and Myra found herself navigating the distance with frequent calls, sharing stories about their daughter, Nidhi. Their love had deepened over time, strengthened by mutual respect and the challenges life had thrown their way.

One day, as she read the newspaper, she was overwhelmed with pride—Highland had transformed into a model state under the new government. Education, healthcare, infrastructure, and public services had seen remarkable improvements, and even the suicide rate had dropped drastically. Her father, once sceptical, now praised the governance that hadn't only improved lives but also restored hope.

As Myra absorbed the changes around her, she felt a deep sense of fulfilment. Her journey—from an aspiring teacher to a dedicated mother and a proud citizen of Highland—had come full circle. Sitting with her parents, little Nidhi, and their ever-loyal dog, Rocky, she reflected on the struggles of the past and the bright future ahead. The state was no longer just surviving; it was thriving. And yet, in that moment of contentment, she couldn't help but miss the one person whose presence would have made it complete—Kesav.

Epilogue

One Month Later

Time moved forward and with each passing day, the memories of our struggles blended with the promise of a new dawn, gently ushering in change. A month had passed, and with it, a sense of reflective pride.

As I sat by the window, holding a couple of old literature books from the college and watching the golden rays of the evening sun paint the Highland's hills in hues of orange and red, I reflected on how far we had come. The place that once echoed with uncertainty and struggle now stood as a beacon of progress and unity. Democracy had taken its true form, not just in words but in action.

My only angel, Nidhi giggled in the background, her tiny fingers reaching out to Rocky, who wagged his tail in playful excitement. My parents, once wary of politics, now spoke of governance with pride and hope. The very system that had once instilled fear in us had transformed into a pillar of strength for its people.

The path had never been easy. We lived through times of political turmoil, injustice, and an uncertain democracy that often seemed to waver at the hands of power. We witnessed the struggles of the common people, the silent sacrifices of the unheard, and the battle between right and wrong. However, in the end, we emerged stronger. The Highland that once suffered under chaos and discrimination was now thriving under leadership that truly served its people.

I thought of my father's words—"Government is for all, not just for those who voted it into power." It took years for those words to become a reality, and now, they were the very foundation of our Highland.

As I embraced the life of an educator, I knew that the real revolution lay in the power of knowledge. Education had transformed not just the lives of individuals but the very spirit of our state. The young minds would shape the future, and it was my greatest privilege to be a part of that journey.

Just then, the sound of footsteps echoed in the corridor. A familiar warmth filled my heart as I turned towards the door. And there he was—Kesav, my love, standing tall in his neatly pressed uniform, his eyes searching for me, for Nidhi, for home.

Nidhi squealed in delight and stretched her little arms toward him. He scooped her up effortlessly, holding her close as if he had never left. Rocky barked in excitement, circling around him in a joyful frenzy.

Kesav looked at me and smiled. "I'm home," he said, his voice carrying the weight of months spent away, the longing of a father, and the love of a husband. I stepped forward, placing my hand over his, feeling the roughness of time and the tenderness of familiarity. "Yes, you are," I whispered, my voice trembling with emotion. My parents watched with contentment, their eyes filled with the quiet satisfaction of knowing that their daughter was happy, that their grandchild was safe, and that their only son like son-in-law had returned.

For the first time, the path ahead felt clear, as if the fog of uncertainty had finally lifted. The past had carved its lessons into us, the present had given us strength, and the future stretched before us like an open road, waiting for our footsteps. Yes, the air felt lighter, as if the weight of uncertainty had dissolved forever.

And, as I looked beyond the hills of Highland, I knew—our story was just beginning.

One Year Later

The sun dipped low, setting the sky ablaze with hues of gold and crimson. The gentle evening breeze carried the whispers of the past as I stood on the familiar hillsides, overlooking the town that had shaped my life. The sun dipped behind the rolling Highlands, casting golden hues over the land that had witnessed my childhood dreams, my struggles, and my triumphs. I closed my eyes and took a deep breath, allowing the memories to wash over me—the laughter and the emotions of schooldays, the warmth of family, the weight of responsibilities, and the unrelenting pursuit of change.

The Highlands had transformed, and so had I.

Life had taken me on a path I never anticipated as a young girl sitting in Ms. Nidhi's classroom, filled with questions and dreams. From the first time I realized the power of words to the moment I stood in front of my own students as a teacher, every experience had been a lesson. Every setback had been a stepping-stone. Now, as I watched the town thrive, I knew that dreams, when pursued with determination, could shape not just an individual's destiny but the fate of an entire community.

The streets were no longer the same narrow paths of my childhood; they had widened, making way for progress and sustainable development. The school where I once studied now stood taller, equipped with modern classrooms and libraries that buzzed with knowledge. The once-crumbling town center had transformed into a hub of activity—cafés filled with discussions, bookstores carrying literature from across the world, and young minds exchanging ideas about politics, innovation, and art.

The Highland had found its voice. The protests, the struggles, the long debates—they had all led to something meaningful. The Highland was no longer ignored by the rest of the world.

Yet, in the midst of these changes, the essence of our identity remained untouched. Our traditions, our stories, and our values hadn't been erased by modernization but had instead blended beautifully with the progress we had fought for.

My parents were ageing gradually and gracefully, their eyes still carrying the wisdom that had shaped my values. Little Nidhi, no longer as little as before, ran into my arms, her laughter filling the room with an innocence I wished to preserve forever.

I saw in her the same curiosity that once burned within me—the same thirst for knowledge, the same eagerness to explore the world. And I knew, in that moment, that my role as a teacher extended far beyond the walls of a classroom. It was about nurturing minds, about igniting the spark in young souls, about ensuring that the next generation carried forward the legacy of hope and resilience.

Teaching hadn't just been a profession for me; it had been a calling. Every student I taught, every lesson I prepared, every story I shared—it was all a continuation of a journey started long before me. Ms. Nidhi had once inspired me, and now, it was my turn to pass on the torch.

Kesav stood by the window, watching the sunset. I walked toward him, our fingers intertwining in silent understanding. His presence had been my anchor, his love unwavering despite the distances and the responsibilities that had kept us apart. Our journey together hadn't been without challenges. His duty as a soldier and my commitment as a teacher had often placed us miles apart, yet we had always found our way back to each other.

Life as a soldier's wife had come with its own set of emotions—pride, longing, and resilience. I had learned to cherish the moments we shared and to find strength in the love that connected us even when miles separated us. The letters, the calls, the silent prayers before sleep—they were all a part of this beautiful, challenging journey.

As I stepped outside, the night sky stretched endlessly above me, the stars twinkling like the dreams we had once whispered into the winds. The echoes of the Highland—the laughter of children, the determined voices of youth, the melodies of songs that carried our history—filled the air.

I realized my adventure was just beginning. There were still many lessons to teach, many stories to write, and many dreams to nurture. Now, I understood the true power of a name and faith, the strength of hope, and the unstoppable force of change.

And as the wind carried my whispers into the night, I smiled—knowing that the echoes of the Highland would live on forever.

With love and hope,

Myra

www.ingramcontent.com/pod-product-compliance
Lightning Source LLC
LaVergne TN
LVHW041702070526
838199LV00045B/1162